Slowly, he inched up the stairs. Then, just as he was about to make his move, he saw the rifle barrel with its one eye staring right at him.

He froze! He couldn't move and couldn't bring his gun to bear on the killer. All he could do was stand in a half crouch and stare at the rifle barrel.

To him the whole scene seemed to last an eternity when in reality it all took place in a matter of seconds.

There was a thunderous roar, and he felt a smashing impact against his right thigh which slammed him up against the stairwell.

Christ! What did he do now? Whoever it was up there he'd have to kill. If he didn't, he and Jill were both as good as dead!

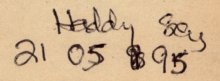

We will send you a free catalog on request. Any titles not in your local book store can be purchased by mail. Send the price of the book plus 50¢ shipping charge to Belmont Tower Books, P. O. Box 270, Norwalk, Connecticut 06852.

Titles currently in print are available for industrial and sales promotion at reduced rates. Address inquiries to Tower Publications, Inc. Two Park Avenue, New York, New York 10016, Attention: Premium Sales Department.

KEY
TO
MURDER
Ralph Cross

BELMONT TOWER BOOKS · NEW YORK CITY

for Madolyn

A BELMONT TOWER BOOK

Published by

Tower Publications, Inc.
Two Park Avenue
New York, N.Y. 10016

Copyright © 1980 by Tower Publications, Inc.

1

A soft April breeze riffled budding leaves on the spreading boughs overhead. A bit of a chill, reminiscent of winter, lingered in the quiet morning air. Melba Stuart, a scarlet cardigan fastened precariously at her throat by a single button, hurried across the deserted campus. The gentle breezes swirled her fine, honey-gold hair about her shoulders. Bare arms protruded from beneath the sweater to clutch a bundle of books tightly to her breasts.

He'll be there, she told herself uncertainly, and the examination is a good enough ruse to spend some time alone with him. She shivered at the thrill the thought of his twinkling blue eyes and dark wavy hair generated. Of course, he'll see through it, she chided herself, tossing her head. A gray squirrel chattered fiercely from an overhanging branch as if to emphasize her uncertainty.

Had she been in love before Jerry? No, not really. There had been a few men in her life. Men? No! boys were more like it, since she was really more girl than woman. She was a farm girl, country-born and raised, and she often lamented the fact that her experiences with boys had not been overwhelmingly successful.

Back in high school, in Pine Grove where she had grown to young womanhood, she had attracted the athletes. They seemed to huddle about her, drawn by the vibrant, golden hair and the soft curves of her early-ripening body. These fledgling young men were cast from the same mold. And, even though they came in a variety of shapes and sizes, each possessed a multiplicity of groping hands, and a single-mindedness of intent that bespoke of collusion. Naturally, she chided herself, she was aware that each bragged of his conquests, real or imagined, and that a single plan among them to pilfer her virginity was as imaginary as their boastful virility. But that each plotted, in his own fashion, to relieve her of that damning bit of tissue, she had no doubts. She had realized early in her adolescent life that her ripe, young body, which had matured prior to her peers, was bait enough to lure the lustful, young he-men on a conquest to conquer. She dated several baleful lotharios, and they soon found she longed for more than strength, a muscular physique, and dauntless intrepidness on the gridiron or the cage arena, and that her backseat defenses were invulnerable.

Maybe that is why she had selected Frankie Rathlich midway through her senior year. She had discovered Frankie among the beakers, test tubes, and bunsen burners in the chemistry lab. His existence had gone unnoticed until that afternoon when he had been assigned as her lab partner. Frankie had explained the rather complex—not to mention frustrating—experiment the teacher had assigned the class. That lab experiment had sold her on Frankie.

She was in love for the first time. It had been so real at first. And, as her warm yearnings faded, she realized that her feelings stemmed from the fact that Frankie

6

was different—definitely different! First of all, he was short—at least two inches shorter than she. Second, he was skinny to the nth degree, and that was a welcomed change from the strutting, muscle-bound jocks. If Frankie owned a muscle, he was careful to keep it hidden. And ultimately, she learned that Frankie detested even the thought of the crushing violence of the football field, and that the art of arcing a round ball through space to drop through a netted hoop bored Frankie. He would have been more at home with calculating the probability of a certain type shot actually penetrating a hoop, or the possibility of X amount of impact meeting Y amount of resistance and resulting in lost yardage.

But Frankie had something the erstwhile young jocks did not possess—a superior innate intelligence. This quality, which had been missing in her previous amours, drew Melba initially. However, time all too soon proved that Frankie wasn't the answer to her inclinations. Frankie lacked even a rudimentary knowledge of love, sex, and courtship. Platonic was an oversimplified modifier to associate with her dates with Frankie. He detested kissing and usually gave forth a long discourse of a zoological nature on the evils and unsanitary conditions foisted upon those so foolish as to imbibe. Equally devastating to her ego was the pathetic apologies he mumbled forth each time his elbow, hand, or any other extremity accidentally came in contact with an intimate or nearly intimate part of her body. So Frankie was left behind just like the jocks.

College was to have been the answer, she had decided. She had left the four corners of Pine Grove for the turmoil of Cape Collins. The Cape was not a large city by any strain of the imagination, but large by her standards. She had arrived at Cape Collins State College

7

convinced that in this strife-torn world there existed but two types of men—those that do and those that don't. There was no middle ground. Nonetheless, she had contrived an image of her dream man—a guy with the build and agility of a halfback, a cager or a shortstop. Yet, this man must be tender and loving, have a mind devoted to things other than sex, an off-tackle trap, a high post pick, or a double play. College seemed a fair hunting ground and, if her phantom lover existed, he had to reside somewhere within the ivy covered halls of knowledge.

Her freshman year had flowed into her sophomore year, with little change except for her adjustment to the laxity in restrictions and the difficulty of the courses. The college men she had met were just a little larger and a bit more practiced than the highschoolers, but they had been either fumbling clods or eggheaded eunuchs. Then she had met Carl Watkins.

Carl could have been all she had dreamed of. He was tall—about six-foot, and his body was lean and hard with a physique right out of a Charles Atlas ad. He moved with the rhythmic, fluid motion of a broken-field runner. Moreover, he was a star halfback on the college football team and was considered to be a cinch to make the Class III All-American team before his career at Cape State was over. The previous year she had been in some of the same classes with him, and even there he had been a leader. His mind was as agile as his flying feet, so he had ranked among those setting the curve for the class. If, during that first year, he had been aware of her existence, he had given no sign of it. Then in the fall quarter, right out of nowhere, he had appeared and asked her for a date. She had been flabbergasted. And, as much as a part of her had yearned to reply in the affirmative, she just couldn't. Carl Watkins was black, and her upbringing made it impossible for her to consider a relationship with him.

Now Professor Jerry Gulf occupied her thoughts. She was in love for real this time and of that she was sure. It wasn't infatuation, nor wishful thinking, not this time. This time it was real! She trembled. Did he love her in return? He gave her a lot of attention—special attention —in class. He teased her unmercifully with his wry wit. Teased her in front of the class until she nearly turned purple with embarrassment. Yet, she knew this was his way of showing affection. He teased others, true enough. But always they were the ones he liked and admired. His attentions toward her had resulted in her minoring in geology—a subject she wasn't really overly thrilled about. She did it with purpose, so that she might enroll in as many of his courses as she could without looking suspicious.

Melba approached the ravine that separated the campus—old from new. The gorge, carved by water, was once a tributary of the river bending along the edge of the bluff upon which Cape Collins was perched. Decades of dry stream bed left the college maintenance crew with a filling task now that the college was expanding. Chunks of used concrete, bricks, and loads of dirt composed the fill. A bridge, with a lattice-work of iron grill lining either side, spanned the open ditch. A thick concrete base housed electrical lines, water, steam and gas pipes serving the new but isolated science building.

Melba was panting as she stepped out onto the bridge. She slowed her pace, stopped, and balanced her books atop the railing, allowing her thoughts of love to fade.

"Whew," she sighed as she glanced down into the

debris-littered ravine.

She screamed! A shrill, piercing shriek which reverberated in the still morning air. She saw, draped across two shattered blocks of concrete, the crumpled form of a girl. The girl's black hair was fanned out around her, glistening in the sunlight.

Melba's books slipped, and she clutched them tightly. What should she do? Panic gripped her! Oh, how she wished the vulgar vision of the naked girl would go away. She squeezed her eyes tightly shut. Then she turned and ran. She pushed at the door of the science building, choking back the fear. The door was locked! Through the glass she could see Arthur Brockner, the building custodian, leaning on a broom, staring sleepily into a display case. She shuddered. Then she turned to follow her thought of trying another door. Before she had taken a step, she discarded the idea and rapped solidly on the glass. Brockner turned to stare at her. His graying hair resembled a wet mop slapped around a wrinkled mold of pink wax. A paunch drooped over his belt, causing his trousers to ride low on his hips and to puddle around his ankles. He shambled in a painfully slow way to the door and pushed it open.

"Yer early, gal. I ain't opened the buildin' yet."

She avoided his eyes which seemed to be looking right through her. "Please, I have to see Dr. Gulf. It's terribly important!" She couldn't tell old man Brockner about the girl. She shuddered again as the view of the naked girl passed through her mind. To allow old man Brockner to see the girl as she was would make the whole thing so much more obscene than it already is, she thought.

"Yeah, he's here. Comes in early ever' mornin'. You just go ahead in."

She slipped past him, avoiding contact with his gray work clothes-clad body.

The science building was square. Classrooms occupied the outer perimeter. The inner core consisted of faculty offices and restrooms. A mirror image of this cube-shaped wing of the building occupied the other side of a broad center hall which joined the two wings.

Melba swung left and rushed down the corridor, nearly losing her balance on the highly-polished floor, turned right, and breathed a sigh of relief. He was here!

She walked through the open office door without knocking. Gulf was bending over a drafting table, gazing at aerial photographs through a stereoscope. Her gasping caught his attention, and twinkling blue eyes met hers. A tingle of warm pleasure swept over her. Momentarily, the vision of the dead girl was washed from her mind as she stared longingly at the man's slightly rounded face and curling, dark hair.

"Mellie, you're early," he said. "Worried about that exam, huh?" He winked at her and smiled broadly.

Melba blushed at his use of the pet name. She felt the fire of embarrassment consume her. It was a name only he used. No one else had ever called her that, and she wanted it to remain his own private name for her. Then her reason for being here came back to her. "Dr. Gulf," she wheezed.

"What'd you do, Mellie, run all the way, and so early too," he teased as he folded the stereoscope. "You really are worried about that exam, aren't you?" He chuckled, rolled down his sleeves, buttoned them and slipped on his jacket. A look of mock seriousness crossed his face.

She wanted to deny the allegation about the exam, but now all she could think of was the dead girl. She had to tell him—someone besides her had to know about it!

"Dr. Gulf. There's a girl. . .a dead girl. . . ," she panted, ". . .in the ravine!"

Gulf's brow wrinkled. "What are you talking about, Mellie?"

- "In the ravine," she gasped, ". . .a dead girl!"

His puzzled frown melted into understanding.

"Are you sure?" She could only nod in reply.

"Where?" he asked. "In the ravine? Who is it?"

"I. . .I think it's. . .Becky Mason," she blurted.

"Becky Mason! You are sure she's dead aren't you?"

Melba nodded her head in return.

"Come on, show me," he said as he clasped her arm and dashed toward the door, running like he knew just where he was going.

She broke free of his hand and dumped the troublesome books on a table near the door and followed his lead. Brockner was still standing near the door, leaning on his pushbroom. He stared in wonder as Gulf held the door for her. She led Gulf onto the bridge and pointed at the body. She could feel Brockner's eyes drilling through her back, and she hunched her shoulders as if to protect herself from his stare.

The girl lay sprawled, her shapely legs propped over two blocks of brick-studded concrete like a woman on a gynecologist's table, feet in stirrups.

A flush burned Melba's cheeks as she realized how the girl was exposed. She ached to run, but only gripped the rail all the tighter and looked away so that Dr. Gulf couldn't see the glowing crimson of her face. Gulf darted off the bridge and started to make his way down among the debris toward the body.

"Go to my office and call the police," he yelled over his shoulder.

She ran, not bothering to look back.

2

Cape Collins is a small town, nestled in a rolling landscape—a landscape carved in a loess bluff which pushes eastward, causing the river to skirt it with a wide meander loop. The town, in its heyday, had been a teeming river port of modest size. The buildings that had once formed its center were spread along the flood plain just to the south of the bluff's crest. The central business district, today, is a little higher up the slope which adjoins the main core of the bluff. The old town on the floodplain is rapidly deteriorating and all but forgotten by the citizens.,

Cape Collins State College occupies a position along the crest of the loess bluff with picturesque, step-like terraces forming the front of the campus. The gorge that held the girl's body had been cut through the bluff ages ago by a stream and now it separated the main campus from the land needed for expansion by the college. But the stream bed is now dry and, in fact, has not carried water for a good many years.

Ira "Pop" Fischer stood on the bridge that spanned the gorge and watched the lab men go about their business. Curious onlookers crowded as close as the deputies would permit, rubber-necking for a view of the unclad girl.

Pushing his crimped, green baseball cap over his forehead, Pop scratched the gray thatch above his ear. Nudity is art, he thought. Now where had he read that? Or had he heard it somewhere? Well, no matter, there was no way anyone could construe that that naked girl in her obscene pose was in any way art.

He glanced at the young girl beside him. His back-alley, derelict appearance didn't seem to put her off at all. The fact that he did not look like a policeman seemed to make no difference to her. She was accepting him for what she apparently believed him to be.

He knew he was an anachronism in Cape Collins. He should have retired ten or eleven years ago. A man in his eighties shouldn't be heading up a police department, even a police department in a small town like the Cape. But he couldn't let it go. It was his whole life, and as long as Mayor Sherrill Olson saw fit to leave him in office, he'd stay. He was an institution in the Cape. He had been Chief of Police in Cape Collins since thirty-one—although it was constable in those days—and deputy constable for nine years before that. True enough his physical abilities were waning, and he found it difficult to move in any way without pain being generated somewhere in his aging body. However, his mind was still as sharp as ever—perhaps, even more agile than it had been when he was a younger man. There was no doublt in his mind that his shrewdness was the only thing that Mayor Olson considered every year when it came time for his reappointment.

Today, Pop wasn't concerned about his job, his age, nor his physical fralities. A sparse man with frail-looking limbs, he moved slowly and painfully through his daily routine. True, murder wasn't routine in the Cape, but it was his philosophy that any time two or more individuals came together, murder was a possibility. Outwardly, the dead girl seemed to make no difference to him. He accepted the death of the young woman as a matter of course.

Looking down into the ravine, his nimble mind rapidly calculated the distance from bridge floor to rubble to be about forty feet. Obviously, the girl could have been thrown from just about where he now stood. Not likely though. This one had the look of a looney. A sexual psychopath who delighted in maligning his victim by placing her body in such an obviously revolting position. Yep, he said to himself, this gent wanted us to know what he was about.

Pop dug gnarled hands into the gaping pockets of his baggy, gray sweater. "What's your name, child?" he said to the slender blonde girl standing next to him.

"Melba Stuart," she said, rubbing her knuckles.

"Hmm." Pop tugged aimlessly at a narrow brown tie, knotted loosely around the collar of his cotton flannel shirt.

"Friend of yours?"

"No, sir. I barely knew her. We had a class together once. Her name's Becky Mason. She was real popular . . .with the boys. You know what I mean."

"Hmm," Pop muttered. He patted the girl's hand in an attempt to reassure her. "Goin' to class early, eh?"

"Yes sir."

"Why? Go early real regular?"

"Not always. This morning was different. I had a test in geology and I wanted to talk to Dr. Gulf before the test. I was on my way over and. . .and I saw her there." She sobbed quietly.

A bustle of activity surged around them. The number of curious onlookers had multiplied within the last few minutes. Pop puffed an old charred pipe as he watched the white-coated men load the dead girl's sheet-covered body into a waiting ambulance.

"Then what'd you do?"

A siren roared to clear a path, and ambulance wheels threw gravel.

"I ran to the science building and told Dr. Gulf." She toyed with the buttons on her red cardigan, avoid the direct gaze of Pop's gray eyes.

"Who's this Dr. Gulf?"

"That's him over there." She pointed to a tall, curly-haired young man in a green suit who at that moment turned as if he had overheard and walked briskly toward the science building.

"He a professor?"

"Yes, sir."

"What's he teach?"

"Geology. I told you about the test."

"Hmm." Pop puffed his pipe, looking down the ravine toward the river a couple of miles away. "Mason girl a geology student?"

"Uh, not a geology major nor minor, but she did take a couple of geology courses, I think."

"She take Gulf's courses?"

"One that I know of. We were in it together."

"She in one of his courses this semester?"

"I don't think so. Why?"

"Hmm," Pop said. He tapped his pipe on the bridge railing and pushed it back into his shirt pocket. "You know any of the Mason girl's boyfriends?"

"Some. She had a bunch." She recited a list as if she had been keeping tabs on Becky Mason. And Pop figured she must have known her better than she said she did. Then she added, "Oh, yeah. She dated Carl Watkins, but I don't think she was really serious about him. He's a. . .a Negro, you know a black boy!"

"Hmm," Pop said.

The crowd around them had dissipated.

"Know any reason why any of 'em might want to kill her?"

Melba shook her head.

Pop handed her a small spiral notebook along with the stub of a pencil. "Would you jot down them boys' names for me?"

"Sure," she said, taking the pad and pencil. She wrote hurriedly for a moment, then said, "Oh, yeah. There's a couple of guys she played around with. She didn't date them, I don't think, just, you know, flirted with them. Oh, she maybe necked a little with them, but I'm sure it wasn't anything serious."

"Who'd that be?"

"Well, there's Kevin Rollins. He's Dr. Gulf's graduate assistant. He messed around with her, but he does that with a lot of girls."

"He. . .ah, flirt with you, did he?"

"Oh, yes."

"What makes you think he wasn't serious?"

"Because he's married. He just likes to pretend he's a Don Juan and all the girls are in love with him." She giggled. "I like him a lot. He's fun."

"Who's the other feller who just plays around?"

"Oh, that's Frankie Rathlich."

"He wasn't serious either?"

"Oh, he might have been serious, but I'm sure Becky wasn't. Frankie's a real nothin'. Of course, he's changed some since high school, but he's still a gross

17

guy." She looked over at Pop who was staring out into space. "I mean he's a real loser. A girl would have to be a real klutz to go out with Frankie." And who knew better than her! She hung her head. "I dated him in high school."

"Hmm," Pop said. He took his notebook and pencil, stuffed them into his hip pocket and said, "I may want to talk to you again."

She nodded and walked away toward the main campus.

Pop sighed and painfully shuffled toward the science building's parking lot where he'd left his ancient Chevrolet. What was he supposed to do next? This was gonna be a tough one. One firm lead to follow, just a list of names. Well, maybe somethin' would turn up if he was persistent enough.

3

Melba Stuart hurried across the bustling campus toward her dormitory. The visions of the morning haunted her, and she felt distraught enough to decide against attending anymore of her classes. As she crossed the street in front of the dorm, she spied Frankie Rathlich pacing nervously to and fro before the entrance.

"Damn!" she muttered. Of all people I don't want to see right now, she thought, Frankie Rathlich tops the list. Indecision gripped her, and she started to turn toward the union when Frankie noticed her.

He yelled, "Hey, Melba." Then he came rushing toward her, so she maintained her pace in the direction of the dorm. He took her arm and walked along beside her. She shook her arm loose and quickened her steps.

"Boy, that sure was terrible about Becky wasn't it?" He didn't wait for a reply but went rambling on. "You were the one that found her, huh? Gee! She was just lying there with her. . .ah. . .with her. . .you know, all exposed."

They reached the door, and he stumbled ahead to open it for her. She stamped through, doing her best to ignore him, but he followed her inside.

"Melba, don't you like me anymore?" he whined.

She sat down on a couch in a parlor just off the lobby, placed her books on her lap, and prepared to try and discourage him.

"It's not that I don't like you, Frankie. It's just. . . well. . .I don't want to date you anymore. Please, understand. Besides I've had a bad experience with what's just happened and I don't really fell like talking to you right now."

"Geez, Melba, you could at least go out with me once in a while. We used to be so close in high school."

"Yes, I suppose we were," she snapped. "But I learned my lesson, Frankie. You just don't turn me on."

"Heck, Melba, I know I was a pretty naive guy then, but I've changed. You just go out with me one time and you'll see."

"No. I think not. I hate to say this, Frankie, but you're just not my type of guy. Not anymore, anyway."

Frankie's face reddened slightly, and he stared down at his feet, studying his toes as if they suddenly required his attention.

Melba rose, cradling her books against her breasts. She hesitated. "Why this sudden interest in going out with me anyway?"

He leaped to his feet. "It isn't sudden! Honest, it isn't. I've been meaning to ask you for a long time."

"Maybe so. But why did you pick this particular time to ask?"

Frankie shrugged his shoulders. "No reason," he said.

She glared at him, and he turned his eyes away. She felt a need to strike out at him, to punish him for all the misfortunes that had befallen her lately.

"Did the sight of Beck Mason all naked like she was

20

get you all sexually aroused, Frankie?" she chided.

His face flamed scarlet. And not looking at her, he nodded imperceptably.

"You've discovered sex then?" She pushed on, knowing that she was inflicting emotional pain on him. She felt a strong, almost overwhelming desire to hurt, to crush him as much as she could. "You know now what men and women to together is fun, huh?"

His face was a dark crimson as her words continued to assault him, but he continued to nod in the affirmative, confessing his sins like a naughty child.

She felt a quick moment of remorse for heckling him. Then she looked him over thoroughly as if for the first time. She inventoried his pock-marked face; his neatly combed but plastered-down hair; the knotted, narrow tie; the bulky sweater and baggy pants. Frankie was as skinny and really as ugly as ever, perhaps, even more so than she remembered. What had she ever seen in Frankie Rathlich? She shook her head. His mere presence repulsed her now, and knowing that she had once dated him, sought his embraces and kisses which had never been forthcoming, make her almost ill enough to vomit. A thought occurred to her and she tried a different tack.

"Did you have a crush on Becky?"

"How did you know?" he gasped, blood draining from his pitted face, leaving it a pasty-white.

"She went out with you, didn't she?"

He nodded, paling even more. His small eyes met hers, and his face turned as white as the marble walls.

"Did you kiss her, Frankie? Did you feel of all of her . . .her feminine charms?"

Naked horror haunted his eyes as he stared at her. His ears were red, but she had never seen anyone, except maybe circus clowns, with a face as chalky-white as

21

Frankie's was now. Suddenly, he spun around and raced awkwardly toward the door. In his hurry he collided with a girl just entering the building, knocking her books from her arms. He seemed such a pitiful creature in his desperation to get away from the torment she had been heaping upon him.

Melba's eyes followed him until he was out of sight. She hurried to the elevator, trying to push thoughts of the past few moments from her mind. The elevator doors opened, and she stepped inside. She got off at her floor, entered her room, and dumped her books on the nearest of the twin desks.

The other desk was occupied by a large, raw-boned girl attired in only panties and bra. She was smoking a cigaret, which she tamped out when Melba entered the room.

"Hi, kid," the big girl said. "That was some ordeal you had this morning, right? God! Becky Mason! But I guess she got what she deserved."

Melba sighed as she lay back across her bed and clasped her hands behind her head. Then realizing what the other girl had said, she snapped, "Betty! How can you say that about Becky now that she's dead? Besides, you didn't know her all that well. . .did you?" There was a note of uncertainty in her voice. People just didn't talk about the dead that way. No matter what they did in life. And besides Betty Landsberg had no right to criticize anyone—not with her reputation.

"Know her, haa! She and I were sorority sisters for two years. I got to know her all too well in that time. She would have sold her ass to any guy that looked at her if she could have stopped giving it away!"

"You were in a sorority?" Melba said in disbelief. Her indignation at Betty's disrespect for the dead girl evaporated from her thoughts. "I don't understand. If you were in a sorority, why are you here in the dorm now?''

"You've got a lot to learn, Melba sweetie. It was exciting at first. We paraded around campus with our boobs bouncing and our asses wriggling like a bunch of little golden goddesses. We were supreme. Hell, it's all a lot of bullshit-nonsense. Why am I here? I grew up, that's why! They make you feel the only way one can be anybody is to be a Greek. Shit!'' She reached for her purse and began to fish for a new pack of cigarets. "You're not in a sorority, Melba. Why is that?'' There was a note of sarcasm in her voice.

"Why, I was never rushed—never asked to join.'' That was something that had puzzled her. She had longed so to belong, but none of the organizations had seen fit to ask her to take part. In fact, it had seemed to her that they had treated her as if she had had a disease or something of the sort.

"You're lucky,'' Betty said. "It should be obvious to you what I'm talking about. You're a country girl and a bit naive—not that that has anything to do with it. Being naive, I mean. But a country girl with no connections. . .babe, you just don't rate. Now, take me. I come from south St. Louis—Utah Boulevard—and my old man was a judge three years ago when I first came here. Of course, he got beat in the last election, but, nonetheless, I was a prize catch then. They rushed the hell out of me.'' She paused to flip a cigaret from a fresh pack and light it. She twisted in her chair to be able to face Melba more directly, swinging long, brown, slender legs out in front of her and crossing them at the ankles.

Melba sat up and rested her chin in her hands. A bit of anger churned within her because of the girl's criticism of the life she yearned for.

"But we were discussing Becky Mason," Betty said, puffing idly on her cigaret. "Say, who was that funny-looking old geezer you were talking to out on the bridge this morning?"

"Oh, him." Melba frowned. "That's the Cape's chief of police. Chief Constable, he calls himself."

"You're kidding me! Why he's ancient. Well, a hick sheriff goes with a hick town, I guess."

"He was real nice," Melba said in defense. "He asked a lot of questions, but he really seemed to care about my feelings. I like him."

"You don't have to defend the old fart. This is probably really gonna rip 'em up. A sleepy little town like this with an old duffer for a police chief ain't gonna know what to do with a murder. Damn! It isn't funny, but he looked so much like a hobo just off the train out there this morning." She chuckled lightly.

"No, you're right. It isn't funny!" Melba snapped.

"Take it easy, kid. I didn't mean anything by it. Remember, I'm from the big city. I'm accustomed to competent law enforcement. In fact, I grew up with it. So you can understand what kind of an impact the law in this hick town can have on me." She took one last, long draw on her cigaret and squashed it out among the other butts in the ash tray. "What'd he ask you?"

Melba took a long look at Betty. Then she recounted her interrogation of the morning. "Who do you think did it?" she concluded.

"Hell, who knows. It could be any stud on or off this campus if I knew Becky Mason like I think I knew her." She was pensive for a moment. "You know of those you mentioned, the most likely candidate for my money is ole Carl Watkins. That black dude lives for just two things, and that's football and white pussy!"

4

Pop Fischer guided his aged Chevrolet slowly along the meandering, tree-shaded drive that led to the back of the administration building. A homicide? He shook his head. It just didn't seem right—not in his waning years anyway. When was the last one? A blunt fingernail scratched over his ear, and he let his mind wander back over the years.

Yes, of course, it was back in fifty-seven, he thought. That time Cora Sue Bailey had shot her husband, Malcolm. He'd come home drunk as was his custom, cussing at the top of his lungs with that sadistic gleam in his eye and had commenced to beating on her. She'd torn herself free and ran into the bedroom and locked the door. She should have known better because that had tipped him over the edge like it always did, and he'd broken down the door by kicking it in, but this time she'd been ready for him. Pop shuddered at the memory. She had stood in the middle of the room with her eyes squinched tightly shut, holding his own double-barreled shotgun aimed right at him. She'd given him both barrels at close range. It was peculiar now how he could remember it happening just the way she'd told it then.

By the time Pop had arrived on the scene, Cora Sue had been a blubbering, remorseful wreck. Malcolm's remains had been a mess, and there had been blood everywhere. It'd taken days to clean the room and make it presentable.

By the time of the trial, Cora Sue had been her old composed self—perhaps a bit more cool than usual but, in any case, she had been able to face the rigors of the trial. She'd been charged with manslaughter in consideration of the crime. She'd hired a lawyer out of Atlanta, and the jury had brought in a not guilty verdict by reason of self defense.

She'd never gone back to the house but had sold it at a bargain price. She'd left town for a spell but eventually she'd come back and bought herself a little place in the subdivision they called Rosewood Heights.

Of course, there had been no need for much of an investigation in the Bailey homicide. Everyone knew Cora Sue had killed Malcolm. In fact, she'd admitted it outright, and folks had sympathized with her. But back in thirty-nine, when Elmer Layton had turned up with a bullet in his back, he'd had to launch a full-scale investigation. It had taken some real detecting on his part to finally, after three weeks, bring in Elmer's brother-in-law, Tedford Robinson. Robinson had been convicted and sent away for life, and after the trial there had been no doubt in anybody's mind but what he'd done for ole Elmer. He grinned at the memory of the accolades he'd received from that one.

But those cases were history. A brand new homicide faced him now, and he wasn't sure he was up to it. After all, he wasn't getting any younger, and it was a painful chore just to get around anymore. Why he'd hung on to the job—allowed Mayor Sherrill Olson to reappoint him to the position of Chief of Police year after year, he couldn't say, except he just couldn't let the job go. It was his whole life now and had been since Shirley'd died. Normally, the job wasn't complicated, and he wasn't prepared for a murder. Oh, he'd probably see it through all right, he felt sure of that, but it would be a test for him—a real test of his abilities. And to complicate matters and make it more difficult for him he had no doubt that the County Attorney, Claude Dale would be screaming for his job. Dale had been trying to get him out of office ever since he'd been elected as County Attorney. Sherrill would have to go through hell with Dale, because he knew the County Attorney would use the homicide as a rallying point to try and convince Sherrill that he needed a younger man in the job.

He was getting tired. More tired every passing year— more tired every day even. He didn't know how much longer he could go on. If only Macklin could grow into the job so he could feel right about retiring—so he could spend his remaining years in quiet solitude. Macklin was doing well, but he just couldn't let go—not yet anyway. The younger man was just going to have to wait awhile longer to be chief.

He stopped momentarily to let a group of giggling, chattering coeds to cross the street in front of him. The murder of the girl was mystifying. Not the murder itself, really, but there was something unusual about it; something he couldn't put his finger on; something vague; something that was eluding him; something stuck in the recesses of his mind that he couldn't dredge to the surface. His previous experiences with murder had always involved family, and national statistics indicated that most murders involved family or at least good friends. Now, he had a homicide in which he was reasonably sure that family couldn't be involved, although a friend might be. Might be? No, most likely was more like it. All he had to go on was a list of names given him by the Stuart girl. Names of close friends, undoubtedly. In fact, the killer was probably a very intimate friend—a friend so close to her that others would be shocked to learn that someone so closely cherished could kill her.

Or, for that matter, it could be someone that knew her not at all. The position the body had been placed in told him that whoever had killed her undoubtedly had severe psychotic problems. He shrugged his bony shoulders. His first task was to find out what he could about the dead girl's life. There might be something in her past; in her life on campus, that just might lead him to her killer. Knowing the girl in life could possibly reveal a great deal about her killer, particulary if he or she were a close friend.

He swung the car carefully into a parking bay and glanced at the sign standing above the curb which read: RESERVED FOR THE DEAN OF LIBERAL ARTS. He shrugged and climbed laboriously out of the car, winching with the pain the movement created in his aching joints and especially in the small of his back. The car door was closed with the tender-loving care of an old man who cherished the machine as a sacred legacy of the past.

The car had been gaudy. Its once bright yellow paint was rapidly fading, and the green top and green spears adorning the rear fenders had been touched up so many times they resembled a green patch-work quilt. But Shirley had loved it.

She had been proud of the automobile from that first

day when he had handed an astonished salesman a wad of bills as a cash payment. It had been a fine April day back in 1954, and he had bought the car for her because she had liked it, ignoring the gun-metal-gray that had struck his eye the moment he had walked onto the lot. It had been the only new car they had ever owned and his sentimentality wouldn't let him part with it. He knuckled a bit of moisture from his eye and shambled toward the twin doors of the administration building.

Inside, he shuffled along examining the gilt lettering on each of the several frosted windows until he found the office he sought. Bryan Turner, Dean of Student Affairs, the gold lettering read. The room behind the door was long, and a withered, elderly lady sat huddled behind a large desk. She was a fragile-looking creature with wrinkled flesh drooping from her bones. Her gray hair was carefully coiffured with just the slightest hint of blue tones. She wore glasses with a gold chain attached to the bows on either side of her head. As she glanced at Pop, she removed the glasses and let them drop to her shrunken breasts. She was the dragon guarding the mouth of the cave, he surmised.

"May I help you?" she asked in a hoarse, strained voice.

"Hmm," Pop said and stepped closer to the desk. "Name's Ira Fisher. Chief Constable here in the Cape." He flashed his badge for her to see.

She glanced at the shiny metal, then back at him. Her eyes were deep indigo and flinty hard. Her pursed mouth was a narrow red slash lined in white. It was obvious she disapproved of him.

"So?" she rasped.

"Need to talk to him a bit about the girl we found in the big ditch this morning." He nodded his head toward the door on his left.

"Oh!" The eyes softened the least little bit, and a frown further creased her already furrowed face. "I'll see if he can be disturbed."

Of course he can be disturbed, you old bat, Pop thought to himself. You're disturbing him right now. He searched for his pipe, then thought better of it as he remembered those dark, steely eyes and their flagrant disapproval of his shabby appearance.

Momentarily, she reappeared still frowning. He was beginning to believe it was a permanent part of her withered face.

"He'll see you now," she said, motioning with a slight turn of her head.

Pop nodded in return and walked slowly through the door. A dean was a new experience for him. He'd never met one before that he could recall. However, the man rising slowly from behind the desk to greet him and shake hands was certainly not at all what he'd expected.

The dean's hair was black not gray, and was cut short. It was neither flowing nor wavy. In fact, it was barbered with a precise military exactness which didn't fit the liberal image of the typical college administrator as typecast in the press. Horn-rimmed glasses nestled over a sharp-pointed nose. He was neither short nor rotund but tall and thin—about six feet tall, Pop estimated. A brilliant tartan plaid suit made him look more like a sophomore than a dean in Pop's mind. Except for the glasses the man just didn't look like a dean was supposed to look, but Pop was not overly surprised. People seldom fitted his stereotyped image of their occupation.

"Good morning, Mr. . . . .Fischer is it?"

"Hmm," Pop said.

"That murder was deplorable! That poor young woman so savagely raped and killed and placed in that simply disgusting position out in that ditch for all the world to see. Oh, what is this world coming to? Why you can't imagine what sort of damage that kind of thing can do to a college. No doubt, it will tarnish our image for years!"

"Hmm," Pop said. The man at least acted like a dean. He presumed the girl was no more than a number to him or a file filled with ink-covered pages.

"Nobody's said anything about rape. How is it you know somethin' we don't?" Pop asked. It was a logical assumption, but Pop couldn't pass up a chance to taunt him. Already, he was feeling a growing distaste for the haughty and proper man behind the desk.

"Well. . .I just assumed that she was. . . She was lying out there like that—naked and all. I just assumed she'd been raped. It certainly has all the markings of a sexual assault."

"We don't know nothin' of the sort," Pop said. "Now, I ain't sayin' it didn't happen but we won't know until the autopsy is complete." The dean was aghast at Pop's apparent accusation. The look of utter disbelief on the man's face made it all but impossible for him to keep from laughing. Pop managed to stiffle it.

"Well! I meant nothing by it, you can be assured!" He slapped a hand down on the desk.

Pop nodded. "Dean. What I need from you is a look at the girl's file. Need to know some facts about her. Especially, her folks and such.

"Why, certainly, Mr. Fischer," he said in a patronizing tone. "Grace," he called to the woman in the outer office. "Grace, would you bring me Miss Mason's file from the registrar's office, please." He

31

leaned back in the swivel chair, making a steeple out of his hands and resting his chin against his fingertips as if to support it.

"I'll be happy to contact the girl's parents, if you wish," he said.

"Nope," Pop said. "That's my job, unpleasant as it is." He eyed the dean for a moment, trying to understand what it was that gave him his special character. Presently, he asked, "Know much about the girl?"

"No. Not really. We have so many students here, you know, that it's quite impossible for one to be acquainted with each and every one of them. Of course, I'm sure her file will tell you a great deal about her background —her life here on campus."

"Tell me about her sex life, will it?" Pop taunted.

"Well, of course not!" the dean snapped indignantly. "Her file will contain her academic record, participation in campus organizations and, of course, a sketch of her pursuits prior to entering college which is in her application for admission."

"Hmm," Pop muttered. He wanted to ask something about the extent of sex on campus, but he concluded that in the dean's mind, sex probably didn't occur on campus. His views seemed to be somewhat archaic which gave Pop cause to chuckle. He wondered if all deans were as egotistical and self-impressed as this one seemed to be.

The elderly lady returned with a manilla folder in her hand, and she hesitantly handed it to the dean.

"Thank you, Grace," he said. "Here you are, Mr. Fischer. Look to your heart's content." There was now a note of contempt in his voice as he returned to the work on his desk.

Pop turned slowly through the documents inside the

32

folder. Her academic record told him that she had been a junior, that she had earned a preponderance of C grades, with a smattering of Bs and Ds and an occasional F. She had been a member of the cheerleading squad, and she had belonged to a sorority—Delta Delta Delta. He read a letter addressed to her and signed by the president of the sorority. It was a copy of a letter of dismissal owing to some unspecified behavior involving her and another member of the sorority, Betty Landsberg.

He dug out his tattered notebook and pencil and copied the name of the girl's father—Ronald Mason—and telephone number. As an after thought he jotted down the sorority girl's name. He glanced back at the dean who was concentrating on some important paper work he had just discovered on his desk, overtly ignoring Pop.

Pop stood. "You want this or should I give it to your secretary?" Pop proffered the folder.

"Wha. . .what? Oh, the folder. Yes, give it to Miss Hackett if you will, please."

"Thanks fer yer help."

"Oh, certainly, certainly. I am most happy to be of assistance in this matter and if there is anything else I can do to aid you further, don't hesitate to ask." The dean looked him in the eyes briefly, then glanced away. "You don't think that any other of our coeds are in danger do you?"

Pop frowned and tilted his cap forward to scratch behind his ear. "There's always that possibility. 'Til we know more about what happened to the Mason girl, you might warn 'em to be more careful. I'll send a man through here more often than usual the next couple of nights."

"Thank you," the dean said. "We'll do what we can

to protect our young ladies." He stood and extended his right hand. Pop gripped it, squeezing gently, but the dean's hand hung there like a limp fish. Pop donned his cap and made his exit without ceremony, saluting Miss Hackett with a nod of his head as he passed her desk.

The drive back to town was quick despite Pop's habitual snail's pace of twenty-five miles per hour. He left the aged Chevy in its alloted space and descended the stairs to the half-basement which housed police headquarters and the city jail. The two rooms which served as headquarters consisted of a large room separated into two parts by a slatted rail divider, behind which was a large scarred desk, a bank of radio equipment, and several metal file cabinets. The door which opened onto a corridor leading to the jail complex was on the back wall. The part of the room on the entrance side of the divider had a row of folding chairs which rested below the windows facing Harrison Street. At the end of the row of chairs was the door to the office which housed Pop and his chief deputy, Leonard Macklin. The door was customarily kept open at all times.

"Any calls?" Pop asked of the pretty blonde behind the desk.

She smiled broadly, which lent a sparkle to her emerald eyes. The paperback book she had been reading went face down on the desk, hurriedly. "Not a thing. What's happening on campus?"

"Girl got herself strangled, I reckon. That's about all I know for the moment."

"Was she raped?"

Why'd they always ask that question when a girl had been killed, he asked himself? Couldn't a girl turn up dead without bein' raped? His lips formed a tight, white line.

"Can't rightly say. It'll have to wait until we hear from Doc Spelchur."

"Is there something you want me to do?"

She looked optimistic and he knew she hated the job she was doing now. Her idea of being a policewoman was, no doubt, some exciting and adventuresome fantasy. Women shouldn't be adoin' men's jobs had always been his philosophy but when he saw he was going to have to hire a woman he had acquiesced. Jill just happened to be the only one who had applied for the job. Up 'til now her duties consisted of answering the telephone and communicating with the patrol officers on the radio. He had not once asked her to participate in an investigation—not that they had many. A usual day consisted mostly of minor traffic violations and occasionally a burglary, and rarely, an armed robbery. Her day was coming though. He couldn't last forever. He'd have to retire sometime if he didn't drop dead on the job first. And maybe his successor wouldn't be as much of a male chauvinist as he was and give her equal billing.

"Not now," he said, as he turned abruptly and walked into his office. At his desk he riffled through his notebook, then dialed the number he had copied from the Mason girl's file.

"What number are you dialing?" a whiny voice said.

Pop repeated the number.

"I am sorry, sir. You must prefix the number by dialing one."

"Thanks a lot," Pop said sarcastically as he redialed the number and listened to it ring.

Finally, a soft female voice said, "Hello."

"Is Mr. Mason to home?" he asked.

"No. I'm sorry but Mr. Mason is at his office. I'm

Mrs. Mason, may I be of help to you?"

Dern! He didn't want to have to break the girl's death to a woman. She'd probably get hysterical and blubber all over the place. Sometimes he wished there weren't any women in the world.

"Well, ma'am, I reckon so. This is Ira Fischer of the Cape Collins Constabulary."

"Constabulary?"

"Yes, ma'am. Police that is."

"Police? Police! Is it Becky? Is she all right?"

"Well, ma'am. . .not exactly. Well, you see. . .I'm sorry, but we found her body this morning. Appears she was strangled."

"Strangled? Murdered!" She was screaming hysterically now. "Oh, my God! Oh, my God! Not my Becky!"

She had reached a high point in her hysteria. Pop waited for her to grow quiet. Finally, only a soft, gentle sobbing could be heard through the receiver.

"Ma'am. I don't like to have to say this, but you and your husband'll have to come down here to the Cape. We'll need a positive identification. Now, don't get me wrong. We got folks here what tells us sure enough it's Rebecca Mason all right, but state law says where possible we got to have family make an identification." He reached for a pipe from the rack on his desk. "And you'll want to make arrangements."

The sobbing ceased only to be followed by sniffling. Then in a strong voice, the woman said, "Oh, yes. Yes, of course, of course. We'll be there as soon as we can. I'll call my husband right away."

A loud click rang in his ear, followed by the buzz of the dial tone. Pop packed his pipe and lit it. Leaning back he closed his eyes and puffed leisurely. Of all things a cop had to do, notifying people of the death of a loved one had to be the worst. He riffled through the notebook some more, and scanned the list of names the Stuart girl had given him. It could be any one of them or a hundred other guys. No matter, he'd have to start an investigation and the sooner he got to it the better.

He smiled benignly. Might as well let that gal out there get involved, he decided. Since he'd first seen her, she'd wanted to get out from behind that desk. There wasn't no use in fightin' it, women was goin' to be adoin' men's jobs and there wasn't no way he was gonna get around it. Besides, it would be best of have a woman question the girls involved in this one. Then he wouldn't have to do it. He shrugged his shoulders and took the pipe out of his mouth.

"Jill," he called.

The green-eyed blonde appeared at the door like she'd been waiting just outside. Her khaki skirt was smoothly pressed with only a hint of wrinkles near her hips—a result of sitting. The uniform shirt with black tie looked out of place stretched tautly over her large breasts.

"Yes, Mr. Fischer," she said innocently.

"You've been wantin' to get into an investigation ever since you've been here." He paused to tamp his pipe and rekindle the flame. A glance at Jill Reardon's face told him she was happy and excited at that moment. It was the first time he'd seen anything but an artificial smile on her face.

"I'll give you the facts." He flipped through the notebook and retold his meager investigation of the morning. "I want you to go talk to the Mason girl's roommate and find out what she knows about the girl's habits, especially her boyfriends." He scratched the thatch behind his ear. "Might get a search warrant and see what you can find in her room. We're gonna need any tidbits of information we can come up with.

Jill stood at attention throughout his instructions. As he finished she relaxed. "Thanks, Pop. You don't know what this means to me. I'll do a good job for you. Every bit as good as Riley—even as well as Macklin could do. You just wait and see!"

He ignored her sarcasm, waved her out of his office and returned to his notebook. After she'd gone, he chuckled. She just might make a dern good policeman after all, he told himself.

5

Pop Fischer eased his ancient Chevy into a vacant parking slot on the limestone-chip parking lot. Laboriously he swung his legs out of the car and pulled himself erect, using the door handle and the door post for leverage. He rubbed at the pain in his lower back, adjusted his green baseball cap, and trudged toward the building.

A tall, gray-haired man in green work clothes met him just inside the door. A broad grin was etched on his craggy face.

"Hi ya, Pop," the man said, leaning a pushbroom he was holding up against the wall.

Pop pushed the cap over his forehead and scratched the fringe of gray hair above his ear. "Danged, if you don't look familiar to me. Should I know you?"

The man smiled. "Depends. My name's Art Brockner. I'm custodian here." He threw out his arms to indicate the building. "I also write tickets on illegal parked cars," he chuckled in Basile Rathbone's best Sherlock Holmes voice. "Might say we are in the same business." Pop continued to frown.

Brockner shrugged his massive, stooped shoulders. I

did a little boxin' once, a long time ago." It was a near perfect impression of the Red Skelton character, Canvasback McPugg, and Pop expected at any minute for him to begin shadow boxing or to swing at imaginary birds fluttering around his head.

"Sure, that's it," Pop said. "Light-heavy wasn't you? Almost made it all the way 'till you broke that paw of yourn."

Brockner grinned and held up a moderately deformed right hand. "Yeh, it was a silly-assed thing. I was workin' out on the light bag, when that sumbitch promoter, Kent Remington, told me that he'd took my name off the card for Saturday night just 'cause he'd seen me talkin' to that bitch of a daughter of his. Hell, I never did nothin' but talk to her and that's more'n you can say for a bunch of his guys. Hell, she was screwin' that nigger welterweight and that's for damn sure!"

Brockner's recall must have been vivid because his facial muscles were twitching as his anger grew. "Anyhow, I turned around and took a cut at him and slammed my fist right into a goddamn steel post. I knowed I was hurt, but I'd be damned if I was gonna let anyone in that sleazy gym look at it.

"I was so pissed off I stayed away from the gym for a month. When I finally did go back, and one of the trainers took me to a sawbones, it was too late. The bones had started to knit and that peckerhead said he'd have to break 'em all over again and reset 'em. No, sir, I told him. Ain't no way anybody's gonna break this hand again. I ain't gonna go through all that agony again for nobody nor nothin. Hell, I couldn't never hit nobody with any authority after that. I'd slam it up along somebody's head, and it'd feel like a thousand volt shock runnin' up my arm. I finally had to quit."

"Too bad." Pop shook his head. "You'd have been a good'un." Pop dug his pipe out of his shirt pocket, and commenced to looking for his tobacco pouch. "Say, kin you tell me where I'll find Professor Jerry Gulf?" He packed tobacco into his pipe.

Brockner grinned again. "Sure. Just turn left there. Prettyboy's office is about midway down the corridor there—number is one-oh-four."

"Thanks," Pop said, holding out a hand. Brockner squeezed and Pop winched. The old boxer still had a lot of strength in that bad hand of his.

Pop watched the office numbers until he came to room 104. He stood at the open door of the office. Actually, it seemed to be two offices. Directly ahead of him was a small room with a nearly bare desk, a bookcase with a half-dozen books, and a wastepaper basket. The outside overcast lent a touch of twilight to the unlighted room. A door on his right was also open, and a light burned brightly. The man in the green suit that he'd seen earlier that morning was now in shirt sleeves, bending over a drafting table, staring at some overlapping pictures through a stereoscope and occasionally making small lines on a piece of graph paper.

Pop studied the young man as he worked. About six feet tall, he estimated. Black, curly hair capped a lean, lithe physique. The kind of man that could make a young girl's heart throb, he supposed.

"You Professor Gulf?" Pop asked, stepping into the room.

"Yes, that's me," Gulf said, glancing up. "What can I do for you, ole timer?" He turned back to the pictures.

"Name's Fischer, Ira Fischer." He found a kitchen

match in a gaping sweater pocket, thumbed it to life and relit his now dead pipe. "Chief Constable here in Cape Collins."

"Oh!" Gulf straightened, looking surprised. "I'm sorry, pop, I didn't realize—"

"Mr. Fischer to you, sonny! You don't know me well enough to call me Pop!"

"Sure, Mr. Fischer. I'm sorry. I meant nothing by it. The name just seemed to fit you. You're here about the dead girl, is that right?"

"Yep." Pop tamped fresh tobacco into his pipe. "Know her?"

"Vaguely. She's been in a couple of my classes."

"Like the Stuart girl, eh?" Pop found a second kitchen match in a sweater pocket and scratched a flame with a blunt, brown-stained thumbnail.

"What does Mellie have to do with this anyway?" Gulf growled.

"Mellie is it?" Pop grinned around the pipe stem. "You ain't answered my question yet."

Gulf stared. His facial features were rounded, giving him a baby-faced expression. The face reminded Pop somewhat of Jim Hart, the St. Louis Cardinal's quarterback.

"Well, no—not exactly," he said, sitting on a corner of his desk. "Mellie. . .I mean the Stuart girl is a geology minor. She's been in a number of my classes. Becky Mason was only using geology to satisfy a science requirement. Her current enrollment in historical would most likely have been her last geology course." Impatiently, he tapped a pencil on the desk top.

"You teach historical?"

"Yes," he hissed through tightly-clamped teeth.

"And you say the Mason girl was enrolled?"

"Yes. That's what I said. Becky Mason was in my historical geology glass." He rolled his head and threw out his hands in disbelieving exasperation.

"How was she doin'?" Inwardly, Pop was smiling, enjoying this interview. Outwardly he was trying to appear very stern.

"I'm not sure I know what you mean."

"Gradewise."

"I really don't know off hand. I'd have to look in my gradebook. I have it right—" Pop waved him off.

"Mason girl have a test this morning too?"

"No! The examination this morning was in paleontology—an advanced course. Like I said Miss Stuart is a geology minor." Increasing agitation edged Gulf's voice.

"Hmm," Pop muttered, puffing his pipe into a smoking cauldren. "Mason girl have a crush on you too?"

"Wha. . .what?" Gulf said, snapping erect. "I don't know what you mean."

Ain't much you do know, Pop wanted to say. Instead, he said, "Stuart girl's taken with you. Shows in her eyes."

Gulf flushed. "It happens," he said. "You know a student crush on a professor. It happens more frequently than you might imagine. It's just a part of life, I guess—just a part of growing up." He brushed a wavy lock away from his right eye and arranged some papers on his desk. "Mellie might have a crush on me as you say, but the Mason girl was nothing but a tease. She was a real sexual con-artist. She flaunted her charms in hopes of raising her grades. She tried her act on me. I almost fell for it—once. Mellie? She's a good kid."

"Hmm," Pop said and ambled over to the drafting

table and pointed at the stereoscope with the stem of his pipe. "What's this here contraption?"

"A stereoscope," Gulf said.

Pop leaned over and looked through the magnifying lenses. "Well, I'll be dadburned! Sure makes them hills jump out don't it."

Gulf smiled. "It does at that. The vertical scale is exaggerated but, yes, one can see the landscape in 3-D."

Pop rambled over to the window and looked out for a moment. The patch of sky he could see from the window facing on a patio was overcast and a threat of rain was in the air. He turned and leaned against the wall, still puffing his pipe.

"You workin' on some kinda project there?"

"Yes," Gulf said, smiling again. "I have a research grant from an oil company. I'm trying to determine if the substructure there," he pointed at the photographs, "is a promising place to conduct field tests in the hopes of finding a pool of petroleum."

"Hmm." Pop stuffed the still warm pipe into a sweater pocket. "You workin' on it last night was, ya?"

Gulf nodded. "I've been putting in a lot of time on it these last two weeks."

"About what time did you leave?"

"Let's see. . .it must have been some time between ten-thirty and eleven. I can't be exactly sure. I didn't hear the chimes so I know it wasn't on the hour nor the half hour for that matter."

"Chimes, eh? They ring on the hour and the half hour do they?"

"Right." The irritation in Gulf's voice was growing again. "They're set electronically. They chime the hour in a sort of musical fashion and there is one short ring on the half hour." Gulf looked at him quizzically. "But you must know that. You've lived in this town long enough to know about the college chimes.''

"Hmm,'' Pop said. "You cross the bridge?''

"No!'' Gulf shouted. "My car was in the parking lot. I left by the back door last night.'' His face was growing scarlet. "Are you insinuating that I killed that girl?''

Pop said nothing, just pushed the cap over his forehead and scratched behind his ear. Pushing away from the wall, he said, "Can't really say, young feller.'' He was fumbling for his pipe again, located it in his sweater pocket, pulled it out and, realizing that it was still full of ash, pushed it back again. "Don't make up my mind 'til I'm sure.'' Pop squared his cap. "You ever date the Mason girl?''

Gulf hesitated. He glanced around the room as if he expected to find an answer written on one of the walls. Knotting his fists, he said tersely, "No! You don't seem to realize that a professor cannot fraternize with his students, especially female, in the way you're implying. Why, the dean would have my job just like that!'' He snapped his fingers loudly. His exasperation was getting to him, and Pop could see that his anger had built to the point of exploding. "And before you ask, no, I did not date the Stuart girl either!''

"Hmm,'' Pop muttered. "I'll keep in touch.''

Gulf gnashed his teeth, but said nothing. He just stood with his fists planted on his hips, arms akimbo as Pop shambled out of the door.

6

Jill Reardon drove her blue Mustang II along the crest of the ridge leading to the new dormitories on the west side of the campus. The building she sought stood as two, tall, twin towers with bases in an expansive, common first floor. The building was red brick and glass, reflecting the afternoon sun. She searched the parking lot in vain for a vacant space, and finally parked in a yellow zone. A neatly-lettered card identifying her car as an official police vehicle was removed from the glove compartment and placed conspiciously in the windshield.

Two sets of double doors opened into the windowed lobby. Facing her was a large central desk area, flanked on either side by banks of mailboxes. A young girl was behind the counter. Her blonde hair was teased into what Jill assumed was supposed to be a Farrah Fawcett look-alike hairdo. The hair could have been attractive except the style was all wrong for the girl's rounded face and prominent nose. She looked up as Jill approached.

"May I help you?" she asked, looking suspiciously at Jill's uniform.

Jill dug the leather case which held her identification

card out of her purse and opened it for the girl to see.

"I'm Officer Reardon and I wonder if I might have a look at Rebecca Mason's room. I also need to talk to her roommate if possible." She rummaged through her bag until she found a document which she smoothed with her hands and placed for the girl to see. "I have a proper search warrant."

The girl stared at the document obviously uncertain, then she picked it up. "Gee, ah. . .if you'll wait just a second, I'll have to get Mrs. Franklyn. She'll have to approve this." The girls disappeared through a door in the back of the office area.

In a moment a young woman, in her mid-twenties, Jill guessed, appeared to her left from around the bank of mail boxes with the search warrant in her hand.

She was tall and slender. The model type with long legs and small breasts hidden by a loose, white blouse. She wore a dark, mid-calf skirt, and a matching sweater. Her dark hair was parted in the middle, combed severly along the sides of her head, gathered in back by a rubber band and allowed to fall freely down nearly to her waist.

As Jill approached her, the woman gave her a careful scrutiny with frosty, knowing eyes. As Jill looked into those pale-blue eyes, the room chilled noticeably.

"Mrs. Franklyn?" Jill asked.

"Yes," she said. "Head resident. You're here about the murdered girl aren't you?" She handed the warrant back to Jill, and she stuffed it into her purse.

"Yes, I am." Jill walked along beside her as she turned and moved toward the bank of elevators. "Head resident?" Jill made a question of it.

"That's right. Baby sitters for the girls on this side. The other tower is for the boys.

"Did you know the Mason girl well?"

"I didn't know her at all." She ran the tip of her tongue over her lips as she punched the elevator call button with a forefinger. "Of course, her name is familiar, but she never came to us with any problems she might have had. As a result I've never really met her. No doubt, I've seen her but I couldn't connect a face with her name."

The elevator door opened and several giggling girls tumbled out. Mrs. Franklyn stepped aside to permit Jill to enter first then she followed. She selected the floor. The button glowed brightly, illuminating the five in its center.

The elevator stopped abruptly, and Jill tottered for a fraction of a second, then her shoulder bumped the wall lightly and she regained her balance. The doors opened and they stepped into a corridor. As they walked along the hall, Jill quickly perceived that the dorm rooms occupied the outer perimeter of the floor. The inner part of the floor consisted of bathrooms, a laundry room and a lounge, complete with Coke, candy and cigaret machines along with a television set. A girl sat Indian style on a vinyl couch. She was dressed in jeans and a sweatshirt, her hair in curlers, and she smoked a cigaret as she concentrated on the thick book in her lap.

Mrs. Franklyn stopped in front of 526 and produced a batch of keys on a ring attached to a chain. The chain disappeared beneath her sweater and was attached to a belt on her skirt. She fumbled with the keys, grasped one, inserted it in the lock and twisted. The door opened, revealing a bright, colorful room.

"I don't know what you'll find or even what it is you're looking for, but you are free to look to your heart's content. Of course, the girl's parents will want to collect her possessions when they arrive."

Jill felt a shiver run along her spine in response to the woman's cold manner.

"Do you know which side was the Mason girl's?"

The woman smiled, breaking her cold exterior momentarily.

"No. No, I'm afraid I don't. You really must think that I don't do my job very well. But, of course, it doesn't involve mothering the girls. Not really."

Jill returned the smile and glanced about the room. It really did seem quite pleasant. She sat down on a corner of one bed. Mrs. Franklyn hadn't moved from her position near the door, and stood with her arms folded across her breasts.

"Do boys ever come to this side of the dorm? Into these rooms?"

Jill received her second smile from the woman. "Of course they do," she said. "We're very modern here, you know. Coed dorms and all that." She shrugged. "Naturally, there are certain hours when boys may visit in the rooms here or when the girls can go over to the other side. They're supposed to leave the doors open when entertaining a boy—but it's not policed. So who knows?"

"Do boys ever come here after hours?" Jill asked.

"As far as I know, during the time my husband and I have been head residents, there has never been a boy in a girl's room after hours. But we are only two people. We don't go in for bed checks. So, yes. A boy could have been here after hours, but such an incidents has never been reported. Like I said, to my knowledge it's never happened.

Jill nodded her head knowingly.

"Is it significant to your investigation? Could such an incident have anything to do with the poor girl's murder?"

It was Jill's turn to shrug. "One never knows," Jill said. "Most likely not. The more we know about the girl, the easier it will be to find her killer." She winced. She was now parroting Pop Fischer and that didn't set well with her at all.

"I really must go now. You go ahead with your search. I'll send her roommate up as soon as she arrives. I do wish I could have been more help to you, but—"

"Thank you," Jill said as Mrs. Franklyn let herself out of the door.

Jill turned and surveyed the room once more. There was a certain ominous feeling about the room. Jill had a dread feeling that Becky Mason was somewhere in the room with her and was watching every move she made. She tried to shake off the feeling but it wouldn't go. She squared her shoulders and walked over to the desk—the neatly arranged one—and picked up a notebook. As she idly flipped through the pages, she realized the book was not Becky Mason's. Hurriedly, she replaced it where she had found it and moved to the other desk.

She picked up a spiral-bound notebook and slowly turned the pages. Sentence fragments in a small, neat, left-slanting hand served as notes for what must have been a world history course. Doodles appeared frequently along the left margins and at the tops of pages. Most were nonsense scrawls which had no meaning for Jill. Then a statement in a rather bold hand leaped at her from the page. "Frankie is a weirdo!" it announced.

It had to refer to Frankie Rathlich, she was sure. He

was the only Frankie associated with the case that she knew of. A few pages more and another bold proclamation, edged in frilly lace, gave her more insight into the girl's character. "Jerry is a real macho guy!" it claimed. Obviously, this had to be in reference to Jerry Gulf, the geology professor. Excitedly, she turned the pages, searching for more tidbits. The next one occupied the whole top of a page and was blocked out in large letter. "Carl is all man!" it read. Jill turned pages more quickly, until she reached the next to last page of notes. She turned the book sideways to read the message that covered the left-hand margin. "Carl is hung like a stud horse? Oh, wow!" Jill felt herself flushing and quickly closed the book. Suddenly, she didn't like the girl Becky Mason had been. She dropped the notebook and rubbed her hands against her skirt, promising herself that she would wash them as soon as she was finished here.

She went through the other things on the desk. However, there were no references to anyone other than the three mentioned in the notebook. Frankie, Jerry, and Carl appeared frequently in her idle doodlings but no further light was shed on the extent of her love life.

Jill searched the desk drawers but found only an accumulation of meaningless junk. Mostly cosmetics, pencils and pens, a Tampax, three tennis balls, and a collection of costume jewelry. The middle drawer held examinations and old term papers. Among the morass of papers, Jill found a small, neatly folded piece of paper. She opened it. Scrawled in an almost illegible, masculine-like handwriting was the message: "Hey, Babe. You'd best be careful of that licorice stick! Love ya, Bet."

The chest-of-drawers contained the usual articles of feminine clothing neatly arranged in the drawers. The closet was also a hopeless dead-end.

Just then the door opened and a stocky girl with an almost square build stepped inside. Dark, plastic-rimmed glasses rested on a pug nose and made Jill think of Peppermint Patty's nemesis, Marcia, from the Peanuts comic strips.

"Police? Then you're here about Becky aren't you?"

Jill wondered if it was an accusation, although she couldn't really be sure.

"You've been through her things, I see. Is there anything I can tell you?" The girl seemed friendly enough.

"I don't know. Possibly." Jill stroked her chin pensively. A gesture her father used to use when he felt baffled.

Finally, she said, "Yes. We seem to be searching for a needle in a haystack—almost. We hope that something we learn along the way will lead us to the killer, so the more we know about Becky the better. I'm counting on you to tell us what you can about her. Maybe something you know will set the whole process in motion." She had taken charge of the room, temporarily at least. "Won't you sit down?"

"Gee! Where do you want me to begin?"

Jill was puzzled. "Ah. . .with your name, perhaps, and how long you knew Becky."

"My name? Oh, yes. My mind does tend to wander, occasionally. Patsy Milan, and Becky moved in with me last February sometime. Do you need the exact date?"

Jill shook her head and sat down in one of the chairs, resting her left arm on the desk. She studied the girl who seemed eager to please. Patsy was wringing her hands impatiently, and her dark eyes were darting around the room. Jill felt uneasy.

52

"Did Becky date much? Did she go out with a lot of boys? Did she have any favorites?"

The girl stared at her seemingly somewhat bewildered, then said, "Yes, she dated a lot and she dated a bunch of different guys." She chewed on a thumbnail. "She did have a few she dug—sort of. Y'know, the ones she went out with more often than the others."

Rather than prod the girl with more questions, Jill waited for her to continue. The girl was staring at her and Jill became aware that she was drumming her fingers on the desk top and immediately flattened her hand against the surface in an effort to hide her impatience.

The girl glanced away and seemed to relax. She walked across the room and took a seat on one of the beds nearest the door and faced Jill. Her elbows were pressed into her knees, and she had dropped her chin into her hands. Presently, she looked up at Jill and continued. "She really dug Carl Watkins, the most y'know, the black football player." She rolled her tongue across her lips. "I encouraged that. I thought it was a fine thing. In fact, I was secretly hoping she'd marry him."

Jill tried to cap her distate by nodding but she knew she had grimaced. She asked, "And the others?"

"Well, there was Professor Gulf. I don't know for sure if she dated him but she sure had the hots for him."

"So, if she dated him, it was on the sly? Secret?"

"I guess so. Of course, I didn't always know who she was going out with, but she never said anything about dating him, just what she'd like to do with him! She led me to believe that there was something between them but, y'know, I'm not sure."

"Was she promiscuous? Real active sexually?"

53

"Now, that's a matter of opinion, isn't it? Sex is different these days. It's sort of like what a goodnight kiss was in your time. Guys expect it. If you had a good time. . .Anyway, why shouldn't a girl enjoy it. The double standard is dead anyhow."

Jill's jaw dropped. Did this girl really see her as being as old as she had implied and did she really believe what she had said?

"Did she tell you about her sexual activities?"

"Some of them. She used to go into vivid detail about what her and Carl had done. I think she was trying to arouse me sometimes, and on occasion she did. She'd spend hours telling me how big Carl is and how it felt up inside and all that. She was really hung up on Carl."

Jill, angry, gnashed her teeth in an attempt to dispel her rising fury and felt herself blushing again and hoped the girl hadn't noticed. She said, "And Gulf?"

"Gulf? No. She never said anything about what they might have done. She never really said that they saw each other outside the classroom or his office. Some of the things she said left a question in my mind. But she may have committed herself to saying nothing because fooling around with students could get a professor in a whole lot of trouble!"

She sat up, placing her hands palm down on the bed on either side of her. "Oh, yeah. There was Frankie Rathlich! She just started that about a month ago. She thought Frankie was a real pathetic guy and she had her fun with him. She seduced him and then crawled all over him everytime they got together. They'd go out three, four times a week and she never failed to make Frankie. She'd tell him what a great lover he was; that he was the best man she'd ever had; that he was fabulous and really made her feel like a woman and other stuff like that.

Then she'd come back here and laugh like crazy when she told me about it. She didn't go into detail like she did with Carl. She'd just tell me, y'know, about teasing him. She was literally torturing the guy, and she told me she was building him up for a fall. She was gonna drop him like a hot stone one of these days when she got tired of him and that woulda killed the little creep. I didn't like what she was doing to him one bit, and I told her so. She just laughed in my face and said that freaks like Frankie were put here on earth to be gigged by the likes of her and that she'd enjoy putting him down when the right time came because he'd got so pompous as a result of her beguiling ways with him.''

The girl relaxed even more, folding her arms over her large breasts. It was clear to Jill where her feeling about Becky's treatment of Frankie stemmed from. Patsy was a female Frankie which she didn't want to openly admit, and her approval of Becky's affair with Carl was, no doubt, wishful thinking. A course she liked to talk, for the shock value and to draw attention to herself.

Jill rose, crinkling her nose and moved over to the window to look across at the boy's dorm. Momentarily, she turned and leaned back against the shoulder-high window sill.

"Do you know why Becky was expelled from her sorority?"

The girl stiffened, then relaxed.

"Not much. She had some sort of fracas with a girl named Betty Landsberg. She never said much about it. Anyhow they both got the boot.''

Jill clutched the fragment of paper in her pocket. She had a definite feeling that the girl wasn't telling her all she knew about the affair but she decided not to pursue it for now.

"Thanks very much for your time and cooperation," Jill said, walking toward the door. The girl twisted on the bed to allow her eyes to follow Jill.

She stood at the door with her left hand on the knob. "I may want to talk to you again. If so, I'll call. If you happen to think of anything else that might help us, please call us."

The girl shrugged as Jill stepped into the corridor.

Walking along the hall, she began to review the interview in her mind so that she would have the facts straight so she could type a report for Pop. She made a mental note to carry a notebook hereafter.

She couldn't see that she had turned up any new evidence. Perhaps, the few facts she had come up with could corroborate the girl's activities and maybe provide some motives for her behavior. She suddenly felt inadequate and very inexperienced. She wondered what Pop could make of her findings if anything. It might tie a couple of the pieces of the puzzle together. She certainly hoped so, but she couldn't see how that could be at this point in time. She'd have to do better or Pop would have her back at that damned desk fulltime and she couldn't stand that—not anymore.

7

Leonard Macklin came into headquarters much later than was his usual custom. It was nearly eight o'clock, and he was normally in by four and never later than six. He wasn't overly concerned about it, because Pop had left him with a fairly flexible schedule. As chief deputy he more or less came and went as he pleased. He had no set hours really. Pop and he just had an understanding that he was head man on the night shift—the real boring shift which in larger cities tended to be the most busy. In a small place like Cape Collins, the town died when the sun went down, and the only law enforcement was usually asoociated with the college in some way. A beer-bust tht got out of hand; over zealous drivers who raced their vehicles or drove recklessly to provide a little noisy entertainment for themselves, their girlfriends, or their buddies; drunk and disorderly or driving while intoxicated were the most common violations of the law that he had to contend with at night.

On rare occasion there might be a burglary or an assault case, usually involving best friends or husband and wife. Murder? Never. People just didn't kill each other in Cape Collins, and this murder that they were in-

57

vestigating now was the first that Macklin could recall. Certainly, there had been no murders during the six years he had been on the force.

Macklin entered headquarters. Carmody, the night desk man, was in a swivel chair, leg propped up on the desk leaf, nose buried in an ever-present paperback novel.

Carmody had been relegated to the desk job several years ago when he had lost a leg as a result of a wound he had received in a shootout. The state patrol had called for help in arresting a hijacked truck. Carmody and Pop had intercepted the truck on the interstate that bypassed Cape Collins. The hijackers seeing what looked to them to be two duffers had decided to make a fight of it. In the hail of bullets that followed, Carmody had taken one in the hip. Two operations, the first with pins and the second with a stainless-steel hip joint, had failed to save the leg. The doctors finally had to take it at the hip, and Carmody had become a one-legged man. He now had an aluminum crutch which he had adapted to quite well over the years. With the crutch he could move as easily and as quickly as many men his age with two legs. But to hear him tell it he was totally handicapped.

The city had wanted to give Carmody a disability retirement, but Pop had insisted that he be kept on the force and gave him the desk job. Carmody, out of self pity, Macklin was sure, had selected the night shift where he would have to deal with fewer people. He was a deeply bitter man and he did his best to make life miserable for everyone around him. Of course, Macklin realized that most of his belligerence was simply a big bluff, his way of communicating, but the underlying bitterness was real enough. And, of course, Macklin had been Carmody's replacement as second in command, and he was never completely certain that Carmody didn't bear him any malice.

When Carmody became aware that Macklin had entered, he removed his foot from the desk, twisted his chair around, dropped his arms on the desk, still holding the paperback in one hand, and glared at Macklin.

"Well, it's about damn time you got your lazy ass in here. You think the city is paying you for all day and all night too."

"Go to hell, Carmody," Macklin said and grinned. "At least I'm not on the public dole. I do considerably more than sit on my ass all night long and read paperbacks." Everything was normal and Macklin's grin widened.

"Yeah. Shit! You didn't give a leg to this goddamned city either. They owe me. Boy, do they owe me."

"Yes. Yes, of course, they do. I don't know why in hell they didn't set up your office in the public library, then us working cops could get our jobs done without having to listen to you bellyache."

Carmody dismissed him with an obscene gesture, using the middle finger of his right hand, then hoisted his leg back to the desk leaf, and buried his nose in his book. The banter was a game they played nightly, and Macklin felt sure that Carmody enjoyed the relationship as much as he did despite what it might appear on the outside.

Macklin went on into the office and sat down at his desk, folding his long legs into the well. Pop and Jill had left reports of their day's activities for him to read so he could be on top of the murder case on the chance that something futher might develop that night. He ran a hand through his shaggy, brown hair and settled back in his swivel chair to read the reports.

Pop's terse style presented only the essential facts, whereas Jill's flowery prose was less informing but more of a joy to read. Macklin mulled over the facts in his mind, trying to make some sense of them. Pop's report had given him no hint of the old man's thoughts on the case which was typical for Pop. Jill's report, on the other hand, was most revealing of her feelings and made her thoughts about the case all too obvious.

Macklin was curious as to what Pop's views of the homicide might be, but he knew that Pop would never reveal his theories about who murdered the girl and the why of it until he felt he had a lead worth following that would take him to an end. Macklin had been on the force for six years and, in that time, he had learned to respect Pop's approach to a case and his ability to reach a feasible conclusion. True enough Pop's expertise had only been expended on burglaries or stolen cars since Macklin had been there, but Pop, no doubt, would be as sly and as shrewd on a murder case as he was on the others. If anything probably more so. Macklin knew that before his time Pop had had a couple of homicides over the years. This information he had gleaned from a cursory inventory of the files he had made at one time, and each time a case was closed a man was behind bars. Pop was a genius in Macklin's opinion. He had no doubts about that. The old man could see things, hear things, and feel things in this kind of situation that went unseen, unheard, and unfelt by anyone else. Yes, sir, if anyone could get to the bottom of this, Pop could and probably would.

Macklin ran a finger over a pencil-thin mustache and smiled broadly. He was looking forward to the little game he and Pop had played with each criminal case they had had since he had become chief deputy. Pop was in the habit of asking "just suppose" questions for Macklin to answer. It was as if verbalizing his theories in this manner made it possible for the old man to pick out the facets of each theory he liked and reject the others, or accept or reject the whole idea. The give and take gave Macklin a partial insight into the old man's mind but it wasn't always reliable. Pop often verbalized a theory in question form that he had already rejected. Why he did this, Macklin couldn't say, but nonetheless, he was eager for the game to begin as he knew it would in time.

The outside door opened and Macklin heard footsteps tapping across the floor.

"Are you Mr. Fischer?"

Carmody chuckled. "Nope. I'm only the telephone operator around here. Fischer works days and he went home hours ago."

Macklin could hear the voices very plainly and he grinned at someone mistaking Carmody for Pop. That was a classic boo-boo. He heard Carmody's chair squeak and he imagined the man shifting his foot to the floor and sitting up straight to address whomever was out there.

"Ah. . .Mr. Fischer talked to my wife on the phone this morning. He said we'd have to come here and identify our daughter's body," the male voice said with a small trace of a whine.

"Ah, yes. You must be the Masons. The man you want to see is Macklin. He's the chief deputy here and you'll find him asleep in the office right over there."

"Damn you, Carmody! Sometimes you go too far," Macklin muttered to himself as he pushed out of his chair and started toward the door.

He met the Masons at the door, greeted them, shook hands with Ronald Mason, and stepped back to allow them to enter.

"Won't you have a seat?" he asked as he pulled a chair over from beside Pop's desk for Ronald Mason. The couple seated themselves side by side, facing Macklin's desk. Macklin walked back behind his desk and sat down in his chair and studied the Masons for a moment.

Ronald Mason was close to six-feet tall with salt and pepper hair. Dark-rimmed glasses with large lenses rested on a sharp, aquiline nose. The rumpled seersucker suit he wore did nothing to hide the middle-aged bulge which drooped over his belt. To Macklin, Ronald Mason appeared to be a former athlete gone to seed.

The woman was still very attractive though obviously a woman in her early or mid-forties. Her figure had plumped slightly, and the black of her hair was too dark and too even to be natural, but both her plumpness and her dyed hair were assets rather than liabilities to her beauty at her age.

"Did you play football or basketball, Mr. Mason?" Macklin asked.

"What? Oh. You're certainly perceptive, Mr. Macklin. Basketball, of course. I guess it was too long ago for you to remember but I was an all-state guard back in fifty-five. I played right here at Cape State. Ah, those were the years."

"Ronald, please!" the woman snapped. She glanced at Macklin. "Mr. Macklin, Mr. Fischer called me earlier today to inform me of my daughter's death. He said we'd have to come and identify her body, so could we, please, get on with it!"

62

"Sure," Macklin said. "I was just trying to put you at ease."

"Well, I don't want you to put me at ease. I don't want to feel at ease. My daughter is dead!" Her voice was rising in a crescendo which might end in hysteria. "Do you hear me, dead! I just want to do whatever is necessary and get it over with, so I can take my baby home and bury her decently! So just get on with it!"

"Gloria! Please dear, I know this isn't easy for you, it's not easy for me, and I'm not sure it's easy for Mr. Macklin either."

"Ronald! Shut up!" She was trying hard not to shout and the words came out strained. She turned to Macklin, and he noticed that even in her grief her deep Hawaiian-blue eyes had a bedroom aura about them.

"I'm sorry, Mr. Macklin. I didn't mean to be bitchy, but this is such a strain. Becky was our only child, you know."

"That's quite all right, Mrs. Mason. I certainly understand how you must feel. If you'll excuse me, I'll call and see if the body is ready to be viewed."

"Ready to be viewed? What is that supposed to mean?" Her churlish tone was back. She leaned forward as if to see Macklin better. Mason reached over and covered one of her hands with his. Gloria Mason jerked her hand away and glared menacingly at her husband.

"I'm sorry," Macklin said. "I assumed you knew that in a homicide case an autopsy has to be performed to establish without a doubt the cause of death and, secondly, clues may be discovered which might ultimately lead us to the killer or provide evidence in court or both."

Gloria Mason said nothing, only frowned and glared at Macklin.

Macklin picked up the phone and dialed. A phone at the other end rang several times. Finally, a gruff, sleep-filled voice said, "Hullo. City Morgue."

"This is Macklin at headquarters. Is the Mason girl's body—you know, the homicide—ready for viewing?"

"Yeah, it's ready," the sleepy voice said.

"Fine. I'll be by with relatives for a positive ID in a little while."

Macklin turned back to the Masons. Gloria was still glaring at him, and Ronald Mason was avoiding his gaze.

"They're ready at the morgue but, if you don't mind, I'd like to ask you a few questions first."

"Questions! What sort of questions? My God! Don't you realize our daughter is dead?"

Macklin ignored her remarks and toyed with a pencil on his desk. "Mrs. Mason, it is essential that we know who Becky's friends were."

"Oh, for Christ's sake! You don't honestly believe that it was one of Becky's friends that killed her do you?" Gloria Mason had nearly come out of her chair during her little fit of anger. Now she settled back but she did not release the tenseness that gripped her.

Macklin pulled a legal pad over before him and held a pencil poised. "Mrs. Mason, it is possible that a stranger to Becky or someone she barely knew killed her, but statistics, ma'am, indicate that it was most likely someone she was close to, someone she was involved with."

"Go ahead and ask your questions," Ronald Mason said calmly. "We'll do our best to answer them. We'd like to see Becky's killer get what's coming to him."

"Oh, shit! Ask your damned questions, but I'm sure there is no point to them." She rummaged through her purse and withdrew a package of cigarets. She shook one out, hung it on her lower lip, and lit it.

Macklin said, "Was Becky a very popular girl in high school?"

"Was Becky popular? What the hell do you think? A girl as pretty and as sophsiticated as she was. Of course, she was popular." Gloria Mason puffed nervously on her cigaret. "Are you trying to imply that Becky was a tramp, Mr. Macklin, because if you are—"

"Gloria, dear. Perhaps, it would be best if I answered Mr. Macklin's questions. You're so overwrought." He reached over and patted her hand.

She turned sharply and snapped, "Ronald, I am telling you for the last time, shut the fuck up!" The last was a scream which reveberated throughout the room. "I'm not overwrought and I will answer any question he asks. Now, sit there and be quiet!"

"Now, Mr. Macklin." She puffed on the cigaret and blew a stream of blue smoke ceilingward. "Yes, Becky was quite popular. She dated frequently while in high school. She played on the girls basketball team and she was a cheerleader for all four years. She was also a member of the homecoming court her senior year. She should have been queen but. . .oh, never mind! I've answered your questions."

"Yes. Ah. . .did Becky have a steady boyfriend while she was in high school?" Macklin craved a cigaret suddenly as he watched Gloria lean toward the desk to tamp ash from her cigaret into an ashtray. He had quit seven months ago and he found that he only craved them anymore in moments of extreme stress or when he saw an attractive woman smoking.

"I sure don't know how Becky's high school experiences have anything to do with her murder now. Oh, well. Yes, she went steady with a young man named Guy Endicott during her senior year but that's over now. She outgrew him."

"Yes. . .ah. . .would you know if she was. . .well, intimate with him?"

"Oh, my God! You do get damn personal don't you. No! She was not intimate with him!" Gloria said through gritted teeth. "I told you my Becky was not a slut."

"Is he a student at the college here by any chance?" Macklin tapped his pencil nervously.

"No! Guy went to State. He's studying to be a vet or some such crap. Can you imagine my daughter married to a dog doctor?" She shook her head. "Well, of course, you couldn't. You never really knew her." She butted her cigaret in the ash tray. Ronald Mason idly drummed his fingers on his chair arm.

"What about college? Who were her friends here?"

Gloria Mason eyed him coldly for a moment, then lit another cigaret, took a long drag on it, and blew smoke off to her left away from her husband.

She crossed her legs and primly positioned her skirt.

"She's been dating a very fine boy. She told me in her letters home that he has made the dean's list every term since he's been here and also that he is a star on the football team." She glanced at her husband. "What is the young man's name, Ronald?"

Ronald Mason winced. "Carl Watkins," he said.

"That's it. Yes. Carl Watkins. She indicated in her letters that they were deeply in love, and I feel certain they had plans to be married when they finished college. He's a fine boy, and I'm sure he would have made her a fine husband."

66

Macklin paused, the obvious question poised on his tongue. Maybe it made no difference to her and then maybe she had never met Carl Watkins. Ronald Mason was subtly shaking his head and staring directly at Macklin. He swallowed the question and cleared his throat.

"Who else did she mention in her letters?" Macklin asked.

She took another long pull on the cigaret as if it gave her the strength to continue. "She talked about her favorite teacher—a Mr. Welch, I believe it was."

"No, dear," Ronald Mason said. "It was Dr. Gulf."

"Yes, you are correct, Ronald. Dr. Gulf." She turned to her husband. "How do you expect me to remember everything at a time like this?" She focused once more on Macklin. "Anyway she was quite smitten with this Dr. Gulf. She said he was the best teacher she had ever had, and that he helped her any time she asked whether it was help with his class or some other one. He was someone she really could confide in, too, she said."

Macklin wrote hurriedly, then he waited for her to proceed rather than ask another question.

She finished her cigaret and put it out. "There was a dean too, that she mentioned. Dean Turner, I believe it was. She said he was really nice and that she could go talk to him at any time about any of her problems."

Macklin waited, tapping the pencil on the desk top.

"Those are the only ones I recall. There just aren't any more."

"How about girlfriends? Did she ever relate anything about her girlfriends?"

"Seldom. Oh, there was one she used to write home about. She even brought her home for Thanksgiving one year. At least, I think it was Thanksgiving. This girl was a real despicable individual. She had the most foul mouth and such utterly disgusting habits. I told Becky to drop her as a friend and the sooner the better!"

"Do you recall the girl's name?"

"No. No, all I can remember is how utterly obscene she was."

"It was Betty something or other. I'm afraid I can't remember either," Ronald Mason said.

Macklin picked up Pop's report and scanned it. "Betty Landsberg. Would it be Betty Landsberg?"

"Yes, that's it. Betty Landsberg. Oh, what a disgusting character she was."

Macklin shrugged, feeling he had taken this interrogation as far as he could. He rose.

"We might as well go on out to the morgue now. Do you feel ready for it?"

"Yes," Mason said. "Let's get it over with."

Macklin led the way out. Carmody ignored them as they passed, seemingly too engrossed in his book to acknowledge their presence. Outside, Macklin led the way to his white Firebird.

Mason assisted his wife into the back seat, then took the seat next to Macklin in the front.

As Macklin swung west into Harrison Street, he asked, "Do you have accommodations for the night?"

"Yes," Mason said. "I reserved a room at the Holiday Inn out along the interstate."

The remainder of the trip was made in silence.

At the hospital, Macklin eased the Pontiac past the emergency room entrance and brought the car to a stop in front of a door that led to a half basement.

Inside was a long, dimly-lighted corridor. On their right was a door and a large glass window behind which was a small office.

Macklin rapped on the glass. "Hey, Murph. Are you at home?"

A fat man, his blond hair cropped close in a crewcut and wearing steel-rimmed glasses appeared from the back of the office.

"Hey, take it easy, Macklin. I'm coming." He disappeared, then momentarily the door opened and he ushered them into a rectangular room. One wall was filled with what looked like stainless steel drawers on a bank of over-sized file cabinets.

Murph selected a drawer and pulled it out. A sheet-covered mound rested on the slab underneath, taking on an eerie cast in the bluish flourescent light. Murph neatly folded back the sheet, revealing the girl's pale face.

The Masons stepped forward. Mason held his wife protectively in the circle of his arm.

Macklin, standing across from the couple, saw a jolt of pain crease Mason's face as they looked at the remains of their daughter.

Gloria Mason stood immobile, a look of shocked disbelief on her face, then she went to pieces. "Oh, my God! Oh, my God! It's Becky! It is Becky! Somehow I didn't really believe. My poor little Becky." She was sobbing uncontrollably.

Mason gripped her more tightly and eased her away from the grisly scene and ultimately out the door to the car. He settled her into the back seat. She was still sobbing brokenly, dabbing at her eyes with a wisp of handkerchief. Mason withdrew his neatly folded handkerchief and gave it to his wife.

"Mr. Macklin, if you don't mind I'd like to go on over to the Holiday Inn, check in, and get her settled. I think she's taken as much pain as she can for one day. Then if you'll wait, you can drive me back to get my car."

Macklin drove to the Holiday Inn and waited while Mason got his wife tucked in for the night, returned and got into the car, then Macklin turned east on Harrison and drove slowly.

"Mr. Macklin, I believe there are a few things that I need to explain to you."

Macklin said nothing, only glanced at Mason and nodded his head.

"Gloria and Becky. . .well, they never got along too well. Gloria was continually trying to relive her life over through Becky, and Becky resented it—resented her. I noticed you caught the note of pride in her voice when she mentioned Carl Watkins. She thought of Carl as having been the ideal husband for Becky. He's obviously very intelligent which comes first in Gloria's mind. The fact that he is a noted football player is kind of like icing on the cake so to speak. And I want to thank you for not spilling the beans about Carl. I saw the look of astonishment on your face and I thought, uh oh, this is it. You see, she doesn't know that Carl Watkins is a Negro. If she did it would destroy her. She pretends at not being prejudiced but she is one of the biggest hypocritical bigots I know. The only Carl she knows is the one in Becky's letters. Other than what Becky has told her in the letters, she knows nothing about him, and nothing would be accomplished by her finding out at this late date. It would probably destroy her if she knew." He clapped his hands together in frustration.

"I'm sure that Becky dated the boy and wrote letters telling her mother about him to defy her mother. She may or may not have admitted to Gloria one day that the boy is black, but I'm sure any relationship she may have had with him was just to taunt her mother—just a way to get even."

They rode in silence for a while.

"The girl, Betty Landsberg. That is a similar case in

point. Becky brought her home that time simply because she knew it would irritate her mother. I sometimes think Becky may have been a little sadistic when it came to her mother. Anyhow, the girl wasn't really all that bad. A little wild, I would say, and she did curse like a sailor. She would drop a four-letter word every now and then just for the shock value, I'm sure. You do understand don't you?''

"Perfectly," Macklin said as he eased the car into a parking place.

He shook Mason's hand, then watched him drive off into the night. He felt sorry for the man but there was little he could do beyond helping to bring the girl's killer to justice. He did understand something else about Ronald Mason that Mason didn't necessarily know. Despite the fact that it appeared that Mason was dominated completely by his wife, nothing could have been further from the truth. Mason obviously let his wife play her little game of master/slave but when it came to the real decisions to be made, Macklin knew as certainly as he knew anything who made them in the Mason family.

Carmody growled at him as he came in.

"Pop called while you was out galavantin'. Said you was to go home and get some sleep. He wants you on days startin' tomorrow. He left me in charge. Shit! If there ever was gonna be a crime wave in the Cape, tonight's prime. I'll answer the damn phone and holler on the radio to them bastards out in the patrol cars, but otherwise I ain't budgin'!''

"Of course, Carmody. We wouldn't think of having you strain yourself in any way. Now see if you can't be quiet, I've got a report to write."

8

Macklin had overslept, but he found habit difficult to break and, besides, he told himself, I forgot to set the alarm. Pop won't mind—or at least he won't say anything—about my being late, he thought. Pop was ready, no doubt, to play their little game of question and answer.

Pop knew that he detested rising early, but he couldn't be sure if Pop knew the why of it. If he were out of bed before eight o'clock, he felt tired the whole day through, and even the smallest task required a supreme effort on his part. Then there was the depression. The earlier he arose the more deeply depressed he seemed to be. The depression, he felt, must stem from some inner feeling of insecurity, although he could not identify its source. And, of course, it wore off as the day grew on so that by mid-morning he felt chipper and ready to face anything. He had no doubts that the fatigue and the depression that plagued him in the early morning were some sort of a psychological problem and if he chose to face them he could dispel them. Since he had risen this morning after eight, he felt neither the fatigue nor the depression. Rather a murder to be solved and his interview with the Masons last night had roused his curiosity, and he was anxious to begin whatever it might be that Pop wanted to do this morning.

A hurried shower and shave, along with a hasty breakfast set Macklin on his way. The morning air still carried a trace of coolness and, except for the bustle of human activity (cars and trucks rushing from one point to another), everything was still. No breeze stirred. Just a calm, clear sky hung overhead, and the sun was already ascending rapidly toward its noontime perch. It held a promise of warmer temperatures later in the day.

Macklin entered police headquarters at precisely nine-thirty. Jill was not at her accustomed station behind the desk, and he assumed that Pop had sent her out on another inquiry concerning the homicide. Pop was sitting at his desk contentedly puffing on a pipe. The old man glanced up at him and acknowledged his entrance with a nod of his head. He was deep in thought, leisurely getting himself prepared for what was to follow. He'd read Macklin's report outlining the Mason's visit the night before.

Jill was sitting in the far corner in the office's only easy chair. Her shapely legs were crossed and she was jiggling a dainty foot impatiently. Macklin's heart leaped as he inventoried her body from the lustrous blond hair, to her green eyes, to her ample breasts, to her flared hips, and then down along her long, slender legs. He brought his eyes upward slowly, undressing her in his mind. He felt a warm oozing of passion spread through his chest, passing through his midsection and into his groin. His manhood began to stir and he hurriedly sat down behind his desk, pushing his long legs into the well.

"It's about time, Leonard. I thought Pop sent you

home early last night so you could be here when the day began.''

Macklin grinned at her, partly in apology, and partly because of what he saw in his mind's eye. She was so beautiful that he couldn't avoid reacting like this every time they came close to each other and particularly if he permitted his mind to wander as it had just now. They had dated several times and every time he had kissed her he became almost uncontrollably aroused. He wondered each time if she could feel his swollen member throbbing against her belly when he held her close. A warm glow engulfed him and he knew that his face was flushed and that his embarrassment was showing for all to see.

Pop came to his rescue but he couldn't be sure if it was on purpose or inadvertent. It really didn't matter to him. His attention was now focused on what Pop had to say.

"Doc Spelchur's report's there on yer desk," Pop said.

Macklin's eyes searched the desk top. Locating the manuscript, he picked it up and read it quickly.

"What do you make of 'er?" Pop asked.

Macklin felt befuddled. He wanted to give the answer he thought Pop was fishing for. He let his eyes wander over the first page of the manuscript again. "Well, Doc was right about the cause of death. I mean the statement he made at the site about her being strangled proved to be correct."

"Hmm," Pop murmured.

"What about the rape part, Leonard? Isn't that a bit unusual?" Jill asked.

"According to Doc, she wasn't raped. Well, at least, he didn't think so."

"What'd he say about the rape?" Pop asked like he hadn't read the report. Macklin knew better. Pop could probably recite it word for word. It was just his way of picking their brains. At the same time, he felt that Pop was testing him on what he had just read. He had expected it from Pop, but Jill? Had Pop drilled her on the procedure of playing their little game?

Hurriedly, he reread the manuscript again, trying to see if he had missed something. But on finishing, he knew he hadn't missed anything on the first reading.

"Doc says he found no evidence of rape in or around the girl's genitals. No torn tissue, no bruises, nothing to indicate that she'd been taken forcefully. In fact, he says that her vagina contained a mixture of semen and Vaseline or some other brand of petroleum jelly. That doesn't sound like rape to me either."

Pop was in the process of reloading his pipe. Macklin glanced at Jill. Her face was wreathed in a mischievous grin, and she winked at him. Ah, ha. Collusion. I thought so, he told himself. It was going to be two on one, and he could blame himself for it, because he was late in getting here.

Jill's grin was replaced by a frown. "Of course, there was no rape involved. No. A rapist wouldn't use Vaseline because that would only tend to ease any pain and he wouldn't want that."

"We got a motive?" Pop now had his pipe going strongly. He had leaned back in his swivel chair and propped his feet on the desk leaf.

Macklin wrinkled his brow. "I'm not sure. It would appear we can rule out rape." He perused the manuscript once more. "However, it's obvious that she had had sexual intercourse not too long before her death. According to Doc anyhow."

75

"If that's the case, then I think we have a motive," Jill said.

"How's that?" Macklin asked.

Pop was leaning back, hands locked behind his head, pipe smouldering. The old man appeared to be deep in thought. Macklin couldn't be sure but he felt that the old man had tuned them out and was concentrating on something in his own mind.

"It's obvious," Jill said. "If she was having sex with a boy and they were discovered—most likely unaware that they had been seen—that fact alone might be enough to ignite our killer's rage."

Macklin nodded. She had a point, a real good point.

"Then which one of our suspects would be most liable to react violently to such an incident?" Macklin could feel the excitement rising. He looked at Pop and realized that the old man was just sitting there listening to him and Jill give and take. He was enjoying himself, that much was obvious.

"It could be anybody, and I'm sure that anyone of our suspects could qualify, but, considering what the Milan girl told me, I would say that Frankie Rathlich is the one most likely to have reacted in a violent manner." She uncrossed and recrossed her legs, giving Macklin a quick view of nylon-covered thigh.

"Becky Mason was probably the first girl to ever pay any attention to him. And if the Milan girl's allegations that she was intimate with him are true. . .well it could just about break him all apart if he found her having sex with someone else. Just think he had finally found a girl he thought cared for him and then to find her intimately involved with another boy—" She paused, focusing green eyes on him.

"What kind of reaction would you have had if it had

been you, Leonard? Wouldn't that give him enough reason in his warped little mind to kill her?''

"Jill," Pop said. "When does a girl use Vaseline?"

"What?"

"When does a girl use Vaseline?"

"What makes you think a girl has to use it? Why not the guy? Why is the responsibility for contraception and, in this case, ease of entry always heaped upon the girl's shoulders?"

She was miffed, and Macklin had all he could do to stifle the laugh building in his throat. She was still trying to play the feminist and that would get her nowhere with Pop.

"Hold on, gal. Don't get yer dander all reared up. Makes no difference who brung the Vaseline. Under what kind of circumstances does a couple need to use Vaseline?"

Jill smiled at his acquiescence, then pondered Pop's question for a moment, sifting facts in her mind, trying to find an answer. Her mind drifted back over her many college courses and finally settled on a human anatomy course she'd had during her senior year. The name escaped her. She concentrated hard, trying desperately to dredge up the name of the gland, then it came to her.

"The Bartholin's glands," Jill said proudly.

Pop looked puzzled, and Macklin said, "What?"

"The Bartholin's glands. They secrete a mucous fluid in the vagina and on the labia majora sort of acting as a lubricant for copulation. If these glands were not functioning properly, the vaginal walls would be dry and penetration by the male would be difficult if not impossible and surely painful without some aid such as Vaseline."

"That the only case?"

77

Jill studied Pop. She was suddenly aware that the old man knew the answers and he was just prodding her to verbalize them. Why, she didn't know, but her curiosity about what was developing was too highly aroused to let the why of it concern her.

"No. I imagine that if the male member was unusually large that Vaseline would make things a bit easier and less painful even if the Bartholin's glands were working properly."

Suddenly, she realized that she was discussing sex, and with males to boot, and for the first time she wasn't embarrassed and she wasn't even blushing. She grinned. A thought came to her. She tried to press it back. It wasn't the way she wanted it but she couldn't hold it back any longer.

"That's it!" she shouted.

"What's it?" Macklin asked, furrowing his brow.

"If Frankie caught her having intercourse with a nigger, that should really send him into a fit of rage," she said. That wasn't right, she thought. It had to be the nigger that killed her not Frankie Rathlich. How had Frankie gotten into her thoughts like that? Obviously, it had to be the other way around.

"You know, I think you're right," Macklin said. "Her screwing a black would be just the thing to destroy Frankie's self-confidence. And from the idle doodles in her notebook, you told us about, Jill, it would appear that Carl is large enough to make Vaseline very necessary." He glanced at Jill "And those doodles plus what the Milan girl told you gives us every reason to believe that she was having sexual intercourse with Carl Watkins."

Jill uncrossed her legs and leaned forward. There was the motive they needed, and he could see that she was as

78

excited as he was. He was ready to go and make the arrest, and she could come with him if she wanted and share the collar.

He looked at Pop as the old man moved his feet to the floor, sat up and replaced his pipe in a holder on the desk.

"Let's not be too hasty here," Pop said. "Theory's a good 'un, but we ain't got no proof. Need to talk to some more folks first. Len, you go over and talk to this Rathlich feller, and Jill you go see what that Landsberg girl has got to say. Somethin' about her that don't set right. I got a feelin' she's tied up in the middle of this whole mess somehow. I'll hold the fort here. Got some thinkin' to do. There's somethin' about this whole situation that don't fit right, but I'll be dadblamed if I can pull it out into the light of day. Oh, yeah. I'll call Doc Spelchur and see if he can give us a blood type from that semen he found. It might be important."

Macklin rose in concert with Jill, and side by side they left headquarters.

9

Sherrill Olson leaned back in the high-backed leather chair, taking a brief respite from the pile of papers and reports he had been perusing. He prided himself on being on top of everything that was occurring in his city. He liked to be ready for the City Council, and since the council was meeting this very afternoon, he was cramming all the facts and figures and extraneous bits of information into his head that he could. This meant reviewing all the material that had passed his desk since the last meeting a week ago.

Olson was a hard-working, tenacious mayor who spent long hours at his desk in city hall. He wasn't necessarily politically ambitious but he wouldn't decline a draft for some higher office if one presented itself. He was content being mayor and he was proud of the way his city was developing.

Olson wasn't an overly large man, standing six-feet-two-inches in his stocking feet. He was a tad overweight with a roll of flab about his middle giving him a somewhat roly-poly appearance. Nonetheless, he saw himself as athletic and sometime during his busy day—usually on his way home—he was able to spend an hour or so playing handball. Handball was his mania, and he boasted the title of "city champion" even though his challengers came primarily from the rolls of city government employees, and there was some question as to whether he won or was allowed to win matches. Of course, there was no doubt in Olson's mind. That there was even a slight possibility that his friends had thrown a game so that he could be declared the winner never entered his mind. Then there was Claude Dale, the county prosecutor. At best he and Dale had a strained relationship, always on opposite sides but never at each other's throats—but the day was coming, he could see it. And Dale was a good handball player, yet, more often than not, he bested Dale at the game. His winning was a pebble in Dale's craw, and he felt Dale was looking for a weakness—either on the handball court or in the ranks of local government. Oh, well. Dale was just one more irritation that must be tolerated, he thought.

Olson had an outgoing, charming personality which exuded a charisma that had made him a very popular mayor with the people. He was currently serving his third term as mayor and had run unopposed in the last election. As long as he maintained his current image, he shouldn't have to worry about upcoming elections either.

The intercom on his desk buzzed. He flipped a switch and said, "Yes?"

"Mr. Dale to see you, sir," his secretary said.

"Damn," he muttered. He pressed the switch again and said, "I'll be just a few minutes, ask him to wait."

Well, he knew it had to come. When he first heard about the homicide he knew that Claude Dale would be making a call. What he couldn't figure out was why it had taken Dale so long to get around to it. The murder was the opening Dale had been waiting for, and he knew trouble was knocking at his door.

Ever since Dale had been elected to the office two years ago, he had been on a crusade to get Pop Fischer removed from office. He had nothing personal against Pop or so he said. It was just that he thought Pop was too old to be the chief of police. Sherrill Olson wasn't really so concerned with Pop's age. He was still doing the job and as long as he was, he could see no reason to retire the old man. At last, feeling mentally prepared for his defense of Fischer, he spoke into the intercom once again and rose to meet Claude Dale.

Dale entered and he clasped his hand in a brief handshake. "Good morning, Claude. How are things in the County Prosecutor's office?"

"Just fine, Shirrell. I hope I'm not interrupting some pressing duties, but what I have to say is extremely important."

"I'm sure it is," Olson said as he resumed his seat behind his desk. "Have a seat, Claude, and we'll talk about your problem."

He studied Claude Dale momentarily. Dale was of average height—an inch under six feet tall, he judged. He had stiff, wire-like black hair with spots of gray at the temples. His expertly-tailored suit enhanced his broad-shouldered physique, and his square-jawed face, covered with a dark shadow of beard too prominent to hide even with a close shave, lent a hardened cast to his rugged appearance.

"What's on your mind, Claude?" He knew the answer but he was determined to play the game with Dale anyway.

Dale laughed, throwing his head back. "You know

very well why I'm here, Shirrell. It's about the homicide.''

"The homicide isn't in your jurisdiction, Claude. The case'll go to the District Attorney. You know that, so why trouble yourself about it?''

"Oh, come on, Shirrell, quit playing games with me. We have a homicide. I want to know what you're going to do about it.''

He pondered the question a moment, stalling for time. He couldn't see yet what cards Dale was holding, and he wasn't ready to go on the defensive just yet. Dale was shrewd and ambitious. That he had an eye on the State House was no secret in state political circles. He was a crusader and would do whatever was necessary to get his name in the press in a favorable light. Three times during his two years in office, he had initiated a crusade against pornography which consisted of banning girlie magazines. Each time the periodicals would disappear from the news stands for a few weeks, then they would be back just as plentiful as before. Dale knew he couldn't stop them from selling the magazines permanently but since the county was largely a Baptist community it garnered him a lot of votes each time he made the attempt.

It mattered not that the one freedom Olson strongly felt should not be tampered with was the right for a man to read what he pleased. Take away a man's right to read what he chose and before you know it other rights would be abridged. He didn't know what Dale's true feelings were on this subject, since he used his attempts at censorship merely to gain votes. He didn't know if Dale read the magazines nor whether he even approved of them, but censorship was not the topic of this conversation.

"What are we doing about the homicide?" Olson asked finally. "The police are hard at work investigating it. We expect an arrest at any moment."

Dale leaned back and crossed his legs. "I suppose that means Fischer is in charge?"

"It does. Fischer is my chief of police and he is the man who is doing the investigating. Fischer's running the show. Is that clear?"

"Any leads?"

"A few."

"Be specific! Damnit, Shirrell. I want to know what's going on!"

"Relax, Claude. We're interviewing the people who were close to the girl. Pop feels there are three or four prime suspects that they want to lean on. He'll come up with something before too long. He always does."

"Yeah, and Christmas is coming too!" He leaned forward in his chair and shook an index finger at Olson. "I've been after you for two years now to retire Fischer and put Macklin or someone younger in the chief's job. We've got to have some young blood in that office, and I say right now is the time to do it." He leaned back in the chair and clasped his hands in his lap.

Olson sighed. "Claude, what I do with the departments in this city government is my affair. If I want to retain Ira Fischer as chief of police I will damn well do it. I don't care what your opinion is, I feel Ira Fischer is doing us a good job and it's my intention to keep him in office for as long as he can do the work to my satisfaction." He slammed his palm against the desk and leaned back, his mouth drawn into a tight, firm line.

Dale came out of his chair sputtering. He raised a fist, then dropped it and walked over to the window and stared out at the street while his anger cooled.

Olson knew it wasn't over. He was sure Dale held a trump card but he couldn't imagine what it might be. Dale was capable of most anything but there was nothing of a legal nature that he could do to oust Pop. Of course, he could file charges against Fischer accusing him of malfeasance in office. But Pop was safe there because there was no way that Dale could prove such a charge. Olson grinned. He felt very confident.

Dale turned and resumed his seat. He pursed his lips and looked Olson squarely in the eyes for a few seconds. Finally, he said, "Shirrell, I like to think of you as a good friend—a close friend even."

Olson shrugged. "Sure we're friends—good ones as you say. I'd hate to have it any other way. You know that."

Dale was staring at the ceiling. Presently, he glanced back at Olson.

"Because you are a friend, I hate to do this, Shirrell, but you leave me no choice."

Olson felt a chill shiver run up his spine. What was Dale going to do? He'd just have to wait and see, guessing was no good. He'd get around to telling him as soon as he was good and ready.

Dale scratched his head and furrowed his brow.

"Shirrell, I really do hate to do this. You won't reconsider? Come on, Shirrell, it's in your best interest and Fischer's too, not to mention the city's."

"I'm sorry, Claude. Fischer is my chief and that's the way it stays no matter what you think you can do."

Dale threw up his hands. "Well, what can I do? I've given you every chance to make things right. As much as I hate doing it, I'll have to go through with it. You leave me no choice now. I hope you can see that, Shirrell."

Olson's nerves were beginning to shred. He wanted to

scream for him to do whatever it was he thought he could do and get it over with. Instead, he remained quiet, wringing his hands and waiting with a blank-faced patience for Dale to continue.

"Shirrell, I'm going to take it to the press—newspaper, radio, television—I'll hound Fischer, and you too, until I force him out of that job. Every day that goes by and you don't have someone indicted is going to be pure hell for the both of you. This isn't an election year but one's not far off and this rhubarb may be just enough to lose you the next election. What do you say, Shirrell, want to take a chance on the electorate?"

He was stymied. He liked to think that he really didn't care about the next election. But he did. Could he take a chance on losing? He wasn't really sure that the mud Dale could sling would have any effect on the election anyway. Well, if the election were at stake, he'd just have to take his chances. The real bad thing about it was what it could do to Pop. For Pop's sake, he'd have to move—take some stopgap measure. Maybe a compromise was in order.

"Are you willing to bargain?" he asked.

Dale grinned. It was obvious he thought he'd won.

"Depends," Dale said. "What have you got in mind?"

"Give the old man forty-eight hours."

Dale shook his head. "No! That's too much time. Hell, in forty-eight hours, we could have two or three more dead girls. No, I just can't give you that much time."

"For Chrissakes, Claude. I'm not asking for much." He was standing now and his voice had risen several decibels. "The old man has been a loyal servant to this

86

town for God knows how many years. He's dedicated his life to seeing that the streets of this town are safe to walk and when things get tough you want to drop him. I'm glad I've finally seen your true colors! You damned hypocrite!''

Dale's face was crimson and his fists were clenched tight.

"All right! All right!" he shouted tersely. "I'll give him twenty-four hours—not forty-eight, just twenty-four—and if one more coed is murdered in that time, so help me, you and Fischer will rue the day he took the job!" With that he stamped out of Olson's office, slamming the door behind him.

Olson smiled and picked up the phone. "Sherry, get Pop Fischer for me."

In a moment his buzzer rang, and he picked up the phone. "Hello, Pop."

"Yep."

"This is Sherrill Olson. Claude Dale has just left my office. He's threatening again—wants you out of office immediately."

"Suits me," Fischer said. "If that's what you want to do, go ahead and do 'er. I'm too old to play cops and robbers anyhow."

"Hell, Pop, it's not what I want to do. You're my chief of police and it'll stay that way until either you or me decide it's time for you to retire. I'm not going to let Claude Dale push me around. It's just that things are going to become unpleasant around here. He's giving us twenty-four hours to come up with a killer, then he's going to the media and air his opinions about you and the job and how I won't act to relieve you of duty and replace you with a younger man."

"You want me to quit?"

87

"No, I don't want you to quit. I just wanted to warn you that Dale's going to give us a hard time. Say. . .ah, any chance you can wrap this up in twenty-four hours?"

"It's possible, " Pop said, "but I doubt it. We ain't got one solid lead as yet. There's somethin' mighty unusual about this one. It's just a feelin', you know. There's somethin' way back in my mind and until it comes out, we ain't gonna have much to go on. But when it does we'll have our killer. I'm sure of that."

"Do you expect the killer will act again?"

"Depends. If it was a personal thing with the Mason girl, I doubt it. On t'other hand if we're dealin' with a psycho, it's a real good possibility. The way I look at 'er, I don't reckon we got a psycho on the loose. I've stepped up the patrol on campus. That's about all I can do fer now. We ain't got enough men to keep a regular patrol on campus. Maybe Dale could somethin' about that."

"How about the suspects? Any of them appear to be psychotic?"

"How do ya tell a psycho? Shucks, anyone of 'em could be. But I'm bettin' that whoever killed that gal ain't one of them psychos."

"I see," Olson said and hung up the phone. There wasn't a chance for the old man to make an arrest in twenty-four hours. And from what Pop had said—and he took what Pop said to heart—there could be another attempt on a coed's life in the next twenty-four hours. Well, he'd have to handle Dale when the time came. He'd find some way to counter him. And, in the meantime, he'd hope the killer didn't strike again.

10

Jill left the administration building and headed toward the science building. She had ridden over to the campus with Macklin in his Pontiac with the idea of conducting their interviews and rejoining later at the administration building. The registrar's office had been very cooperative and had supplied them with class schedules for each of the two students. According to Betty Landsberg's schedule, she was supposed to be in an anatomy class on the second floor of the science building.

As she crossed the bridge spanning the river, Jill stopped to view the littered bottom of the dry stream course. She tried to imagine the murdered girl as Pop had described her lying across the brick-studded concrete fragments. She shuddered at the sight her mind conjured up and turned away.

She was a bit confused. True, she knew very little about police work, but Pop's methods did seem to be a bit amateurish, as if the old man didn't know what he was doing exactly. The only effort he had made to question any of the prime suspects was his interrogation of the geology professor and, now, assigning her to interview the Landsberg girl, and Macklin to interrogate the

Rathlich kid. He seemed to have no direction and what he was doing he was doing painfully slow. Oh, well, maybe the old man knew what he was about, but she was still skeptical.

The investigation brought to mind memories of her father—memories that were, for the most part, painful. Nonetheless, she allowed them to roll over her, mixing the good thoughts with the bad. He'd been a patrolman in Flint, Michigan where she had grown to young womanhood. She could recall the pungent odor of his blue woolen uniform when he'd come in after a rain storm or after it had snowed during the winter. She could remember running to him and his big arms hugging her tight, and the nighttime sessions when he'd tell her stories of the more whimsical side of his being a policeman. And, as always, when she thought of him, she reviewed his death in her mind.

It had been only two weeks before she was to graduate from high school. He'd been gunned down by two blacks during a robbery of a liquor store on Detroit Street.

They had used a sawed-off shotgun, and Jill had never gotten to see his body. It was a closed casket funeral.

The agony of her grief had turned her into a walking zombie for the better part of that summer. She retained a hazy memory of her commencement exercises, and the summer was little more than a bad dream she had tried to forget. It was well into August before she felt reasonably normal again and was able to resume her life on a fulltime basis. Most of the grief and pain had gone and she had tried not to think of her loss. She had blamed herself because she had been rather spiteful toward him because he had refused her permission to go to a concert in Detroit, and she had never seen him again.

If she blamed herself she blamed the blacks more. She never learned who they were, they killed her father, so she blamed all blacks—a whole race condemned. Her hatred had grown and she had nourished it and watched it flower into full bloom. Now she had a chance to vent that hatred, to direct her anger toward a man she hated but had not yet met. She hated him simply because he was black.

She brushed a tear from her eye and looked at the glass doors of the science building. She clasped a handle, pulled it open and stepped inside. A blast of cold air hit her and she shivered slightly but was nonetheless relieved to be in out of the uncommon afternoon heat of early spring. She glanced at the copy of the Landsberg girl's schedule once more. According to it Betty Landsberg should be on the second floor in room 215.

The stairs were mid-way down the central corridor and upon reaching the second floor she saw an elderly man leaning on a pushbroom, apparently reading scraps of information from a cork bulletin board. His watery eyes surveyed her figure carefully, then flicked back to look her in the eyes, a twist of a smile trembling at the corners of his mouth.

"Can I help you, Miss?" he asked.

The voice made her feel uncomfortable. There was something about it that was familiar. She was sure she had heard it before but she couldn't think where. Most peculiar was the fact that the old man there before her was a complete stranger and yet that something about his voice still stirred thoughts of familiarity. Why, she couldn't say nor even guess. She knew she had never seen him before, that she could recall, yet why was his voice so familiar? She shook her head and said, "Yes.

I'm looking for Anatomy 421. It's supposed to be in room 215.

"Yep, that's right. That'll be Dr. Parsons's course. But what's a police lady want with a science class?"

This time the voice was different, but still familiar. She was more confused than ever now. It was almost like two different people had addressed her but that wasn't possible because the old man was the only other person in the hall. But just to be sure, she looked around.

"I'm looking for a student. Ah. . .Betty Landsberg," she said.

"She in trouble with the law, is she?" he asked.

"No. Nothing like that. I just want to ask her a few routine questions about her relationship with the girl who was killed yesterday."

"I see," he said, scratching his chin. "Well, then just follow me. I'll see she gets the message."

His gait reminded her of an ice skater's. His feet splayed out to the side as he walked. The stench of rotten eggs struck her nostrils as they turned a corner and she coughed.

"Chemistry lab," he said in way of an explanation. "Some kind of sulfur compound they fool around with in there. You work for Pop Fischer?"

She nodded.

"Yep. Me and him are good friends. We go back a long ways."

"Oh!" Jill said, her mouth forming a big surprised O.

He said no more. Apparently he wasn't going to elaborate on his friendship with Pop—not to her at least.

They stopped in front of 215 and the old man rapped solidly on the door. A tall, buxom woman with tightly-curled blond hair, obviously a bit perturbed, poked her head out of the door.

"What is it, Art?" she asked.

"Police lady here wants to see Betty Landsberg, Dr. Parsons. She's supposed to be in your class."

"That's right, she is. I'll send her right out."

The woman closed the door. The old man grinned at Jill as if waiting for praise for a job well done. "If you need anything more, I'll be around. Name's Art Brockner."

"Oh, thanks. Thanks very much for your trouble. I certainly appreciate it."

He squeezed her hand gently and walked away in his odd skating motion.

Momentarily the classroom door opened and a puzzled young coed appered. Jill looked her over and decided she wasn't at all pretty. Raw-boned and lanky with narrow, boyish hips, and she wore her hair clipped in a mannish style.

"Are you Betty Landsberg?" Jill asked.

"Yeah, that's me. What can I do for you?"

"Is there somewhere we can talk?"

"Sure. The girls' john has got a lounge. It's not exactly private but there won't be a rush until the period ends. We got a half hour or so." She started down the corridor, then turned and spoke over her shoulder. "This is about Becky Mason isn't it?"

"It is," Jill said as she walked down the corridor with the girl, around a corner and into the ladies room. Inside, there was a couch and two easy chairs covered in vinyl. An artificial plant reposed on a square end table near the couch. Jill sat in one of the chairs while Betty Landsberg plopped down onto the couch, tossing her books aside. She dug in her purse, pulled out a plastic cigaret case, extracted a cigaret, tapped it on a red-painted thumbnail, and lit it with a plastic, throw-away lighter. The painted fingernails seemed to be her only concession to feminity.

"You and Becky Mason were sorority sisters weren't you?" Jill asked.

"Yeah. We were sisters and roommates for a while for that matter. So what?"

"Well. . ." Jill paused. How did she pursue the line of questioning she had in mind? The girl was obviously belligerent, and Jill didn't want trouble from her. "What. . .ah. . .was your relationship with Becky like?"

"Good. Shit, we got along real good. We didn't have any trouble or we wouldn't have had any trouble if that asshole of a house mother had stayed out of it."

"We know that you and Becky were released from the sorority at the same time. Why was that?" Jill stroked her jaw.

"Released. Haa! You really want to know?" Betty took her time crushing her cigaret in an ashtray.

"Yes. For some reason I feel it has to be pertinent to this case."

"Uh, oh. Well, don't say I didn't warn you. You see, lady, it was this way. Me and Becky were lovers, y'know. What I'm tryin' to say is that I'm a lesbian, and that shit-ass of a house mother walked into our room one day and caught us makin' out. You know, a little sixty-nine. Now, she didn't have no right bustin' up our privacy, you know what I mean. Hell, I mean what we did in those rooms was our business. But, anyhow, we got the boot. The old bitch called us a couple of perverts." She fished another cigaret from the case and lit it quickly, crossing her blue-jean-covered legs.

Jill's face was flaming. She was mortified and didn't really know what to do next. "Was. . .was. . .Becky a . . .er. . .ah. . .a lesbian too?"

"Shit no!" she laughed. "Becky was AC/DC, you know, bi. She liked doin' it with me but she also liked it with guys, especially that nigger asshole, Carl Watkins. Man, he's got a wang that hangs halfway to his knees. He had his nerve too. I walked in on them one time right there in the sorority house, and Carl was humpin' the hell out of her. If the house mother had caught them that time instead of me. Wow!"

Jill had gained control of her emotions now and the embarrassment had fled. A tinge of anger, emanating from the girl's use of profanity had replaced it.

"Were you jealous, Betty?"

"Jealous? Me? Hell, no!" She flicked ashes into the ashtray.

"I think you were jealous. You didn't like competing with a nigger football star now did you?" Jill was taunting her. She wanted company. She wanted this girl to hate that nigger as much as she did.

"Okay. Okay. So I didn't like her screwing around with Carl or that ugly little snit, Frankie either." She took a long drag on her cigaret and stared Jill calmly in the eyes. "If you want my opinion as to who done her in, it was that nigger bastard. She dropped him a couple of weeks ago and that really hurt his ego. He likes white girls but it sure busted him up when one of his white chicks gave him the dump."

Jill felt smug and grinned triumphantly. The girl was accusing Watkins and that suited her just fine. She liked to believe that she was more than ever sure that Carl Watkins was the man.

"How about you, Betty? How were you and Betty

95

getting along since you left the sorority?"

"So-so, I guess. We haven't done much but speak if we happen to run into each other since we got kicked out of the sorority. And that's been like a year."

"Were you in love with her?" The girl's reaction told Jill that she'd touched a tender nerve.

Betty sniffed. "Hell, yes, I was in love with her. What did you expect?" She hung her head and Jill was sure she saw a tear at the corner of her eye. Then suddenly she broke into great wracking sobs and buried her head in her arms on the arm of the couch and cried.

Jill leaned forward and patted her on the head. "Betty, did you kill Becky?" She spoke in a soft, tender voice.

The girl reared up. Her eyes were red and her cheeks were stained with tears. "No. No. Oh, hell, no. I didn't kill Becky. You gotta believe me, I didn't kill her. I loved her. I couldn't hurt her. No way. Even when I thought she deserved it, I couldn't hurt her. I didn't kill her. Please, believe me, I didn't kill her."

"That's all right," Jill said and patted her hand. "I believe you, but I may need to talk to you again. Anyway, thanks for answering my questions. I really appreciate it."

Jill had gathered up her purse and walked into the hall. If Betty had caught Becky copulating with Watkins once, it could have happened again. And, in her obviously twisted mind, killing Becky was entirely feasible. For an instant she had almost believed that Betty hadn't done it. And that was the way she wanted it. Carl Watkins had to be the one to pay for the killing—both Becky's and her father's. Her eyes were burning and she rubbed a knuckle through them. But now she wasn't so sure. Betty certainly had a motive and committing murder wasn't out of character for her. Jill felt sure of that.

As suddenly as he had left, Jill turned back and caught Betty just as she was coming out of the lounge. Except for a thin rim of redness around each eye, it would be difficult to see that the girl had been crying so hard just a few minutes previous.

"What now?" Betty asked.

"I'm sorry to both you further but I just thought of something else you might help me with—answer a question or two more."

"All right," she said resignedly.

"Are there any others she was close to?"

She looked at Jill with a bland expression and pursed her lips, then grinned provocatively.

"Shit, yeah. But you don't mean who she was close to, you mean, y'know, who else was she screwing! You got a pencil? I'll give you a list."

Jill reached for her purse but remembered that she had not as yet had time to purchase a notebook. She found a pen and glanced at Betty Landsberg as she crossed her legs to provide a better writing surface. The girl's eyes followed her hemline much as a man's would when an attractive woman in a skirt crossed her legs. Jill glared at her.

"I don't seem to have any paper to write on." Her voice was clipped and stern.

Betty tore a page from a notebook and handed it to her.

"I thought all cops carried notebooks." She was smirking, Jill noticed, but she took the paper and waited, pen poised.

"Okay. There's Carl and Frankie that I told you about. Then there's Kevin Rollins and Dr. Gulf—"

"Are you sure about Professor Gulf?"

"Shit yeah. I'm sure."

"And you know for a fact that she had intercourse with each of these?" Her pen raced over the paper.

"Yeah." Betty laughed. "She was screwin' each and every one real regular and that's not to mention a glob of one-night stands. But Carl, he was her favorite."

A bell rang somewhere, grating on Jill's nerves like a broken fingernail drawn across a chalkboard. Presently, the door opened and several girls came in whispering and gesturing to one another.

"Well, lady. It looks like this is the end of your interrogation. We can't get any quiet in here as long as these simpering freshmen are parading in and out."

Jill doubted they were all freshmen and they certainly were not simpering. "I guess that's all I need for now. I'll be in touch." She decided against completing the list. For some reason she didn't feel she could rely on what Betty Landsberg was telling her. She had a strong premonition that she was lying about Professor Gulf and Kevin Rollins.

"I bet you will," Betty Landsberg said, hastily lighting another cigaret.

11

Macklin left the administration building and headed for Owen Hall. Urgency tugged at him and he broke into a long-strided pace which stretched his long legs to their utmost. The pace, which was his normal gait when walking, ate up the distance very rapidly and he soon stood at the doors of Owen Hall.

The dirty brick building was set near the crest of the loessal ridge and was a part of the old campus. Owen Hall had been there as far back as he could remember even in those early days when his father had brought him to town from their farm and drove around the winding campus streets showing him the sights. Undoubtedly, had he not lived within commuting distance from the campus, he himself would have been a resident at Owen Hall when he had attended Cape State College.

The heavy door creaked as he tugged it open. The interior was cool and dim, leaving too many unwanted shadows in the broad hall which led from the front doors all the way through the building to the back doors. He stepped inside and paused momentarily to allow his eyes to adjust to the dark interior. An L-shaped desk with a long-haired boy behind it was on his right.

"I'm Officer Macklin." He addressed the youth behind the desk. "I'd like to talk with Frank Rathlich. Could you tell me if he's in?"

The youth's expression didn't change. Apparently he wasn't impressed by a policeman's uniform. He brushed a stray hank of hair out of his eyes. His crooked nose had obviously been broken some time in the past and never set properly. A small scar decorated the point of his chin. It was in a place where it might have been the result of a fall, a shaky shaving hand or a hard-knuckled fist.

"Yeah. Just a minute and I'll check an' see if he's in." The boy walked to the call station, punched a button and talked into the transmitter. Abruptly he turned, his hand still on the lever. "You want to go up to the room or do you want him to come down here?" He swung his head, but was unsuccessful in getting the stray lock of hair out of his eyes.

Macklin pondered the boy's question for a moment, then said. "Tell him to come down. I'll be over in that little alcove over there." He pointed to the center arch along the hall.

The alcove was furnished with a vinyl-covered couch and two matching chairs. Macklin took a seat on one end of the sofa. In a few moments a very skinny youth in baggy corduroy trousers and crewneck sweater appeared.

"You're Frank Rathlich?" Macklin asked.

The boy nodded. His pock-marked face was an unhealthy-looking pasty-white and he was wringing his hands in a state of high agitation. Macklin gestured toward the chair nearest his position on the end of the sofa. The boy glanced down, then moved over and perched on the edge of the chair, gripping the arms with white-knuckled fists.

"Frank, I'm sure you must be aware that Rebecca Mason was killed night before last and that her body was found here on campus." The boy nodded, and Macklin continued. "We have information that you were a friend of hers, Frank, and I'd like to ask you a few questions about your relationship with her, if you don't mind?"

The youth's face paled noticeably and he commenced to wringing his hands once more. He nodded, then shoved himself back into the chair and once more took his lock grip on the chair arms.

Macklin leaned forward, grasping his left wrist with his right hand just over his belt buckle. The lad shrank back into the chair still further.

"You dated Becky Mason, didn't you?" Macklin asked.

Frank gulped, cleared his throat, then said in a broken voice which oscilated between bass and tenor. "It was more than that. We were going to get engaged as soon as I had saved up enough money to buy the ring."

"You were close then?"

"Oh yes. We were very much in love." He gulped.

Macklin leaned back, twisting a ring on his right hand.

"Were you intimate with her, Frank?"

"Intimate? I. . .I don't know what you mean."

Macklin grimaced. What was the kid trying to pull. He was obviously very bright—naive maybe, but bright. "Did you have sex with her, Frank?"

His face turned deathly white again, and for a moment Macklin thought the kid was going to pass out. Finally, he hung his head and nodded.

"Where and when, Frank?"

He looked up at Macklin. There were tears in his eyes.

"Honest, Mister, I didn't kill Becky," he said in a trembling voice.

"I didn't say you did, Frank. I just want to find out about Becky Mason. What she was like. Who her friends were, and who her enemies might have been—if she had any—and apparently she did. To do this I have to ask you questions, Frank, and you have to answer the questions truthfully. Don't be frightened, Frank. I have to do this. I'm investigating a homicide and, unfortunately, Frank, your relationship with the dead girl makes you a part of it for now."

The kid hung his head again. "I can tell you what she was like, but I don't know much about her friends. We never talked about it. She kinda liked that black football player, but I don't know anybody that was her enemy. She was really a sweet girl. I liked her a lot—no, I loved her a lot."

"That's fine, Frank, but where did you and Becky go when you had sex together?"

He was shaking visibly now and holding on to the chair with every ounce of strength he could muster. "We did it in the bushes, out in the fields, and once in a while in a car."

"Do you have a car, Frank?"

"No, sir. Becky'd borrow one from a friend of hers every so often. Then we'd go to a drive-in movie or out in the country. We'd sit there and talk and kiss for a long time, then we'd do it and come back to the dorm."

"Who'd Becky borrow the car from?"

"A girl she said. The only girl friend that I knew of. Her name's Betty Landsberg. I guess she was a real good friend of Becky's. In fact, Becky was going to have her for a bridesmaid when we got married."

It was Macklin's turn to gulp. He rubbed his eyes and

remembered Jill's report and what Patsy Milan had had to say. Christ, but this kid was gullible, extremely gullible as well as being naive. From what they had dug up so far, he'd gotten the idea that Becky Mason wasn't on the best of terms with the Landsberg girl. Maybe he'd misinterpreted something along the way. He'd have to wait and see what Jill had found out in her questioning of Betty Landsberg. Macklin crossed his legs and longed for a cigaret.

"Did you go out with Becky Tuesday night, Frank?"

"Honest, Mister, I didn't do it! I didn't do it!" He was sobbing now, unable to hold back the fear or pain whichever it was.

"Hey, take it easy, Frank. I just want to know if you took her out on Tuesday. I didn't intend for you to interpret it as an accusation."

Glancing up, Rathlich nodded with tears streaming down his face. He gulped, sniffed, and wiped the back of his hand across his nose. "Yes, we went out."

"Where'd you go, Frank?"

"To a movie." He sniffled and wiped the back of his hand across his nose again. "Then we went to McDonald's for a hamburger and a shake. Then I took her back to her dorm."

"What time did you get back?"

"It was about ten-thirty. She didn't have to be in until twelve but she wanted to study for a test so she went in early."

It checked. She more than likely had a second date for that night after Frank brought her to the dorm. Or Frankie could be lying about getting her in. Well? From the looks of the kid, he was telling the truth, if he could bank on looks. Yes, it was very likely that she sneaked out to meet her killer after Rathlich had brought her in.

Macklin gritted his teeth. He hated to ask the question, but he knew he had to. He folded his hands and hooked his thumbs under his chin.

"Did you have sex with her Tuesday night, Frank?"

He was sobbing more violently now and he nodded his head.

"Where, Frank?"

"Under the bridge," he sobbed. "We got a little place fixed up under a piece of concrete where we can't. . . .er.
. .couldn't be seen."

Damn! The kid made it impossible for him to believe one way or the other. Under the bridge! He had to be naive. Was he aware of what his confession was doing to his credibility? Then it struck Macklin. Who had been watching them on Tuesday? If the killer had been watching the girl and Rathlich—damn, it made Jill's theory right on. Of course, the killer saw her give herself to Frank, then after Frank took her home the killer called her out again and strangled her. But who? That was the question. It had to be someone she was on good terms with—someone she would sneak out to see. Watkins was a good possibility but, then so was everyone else on the list. Well, he might as well proceed and see what other clues this quivering kid might reveal.

"Did you use Vaseline, Frank?"

"Vaseline? Whatever for?" There was a puzzled expression lining his face.

"Did you use a rubber by any chance?"

"A rubber? Heck, no. Becky was on the pill. We didn't have to worry about her getting pregnant."

"Okay, Frank, we'll be in touch." He rose and started to leave.

"Wait!" the kid screamed. "You don't still think I did it, do you?" He was still quivering like a frightened rabbit, and his face remained a pasty-white.

Macklin turned and looked sternly at the boy for a minute. Then he grinned. "No, Frank. I don't think you did it." Macklin was rewarded with a smile. He was glad now that he had set the boy's mind at ease.

Macklin hurried toward the administration building to meet Jill, wondering what she had found out from the Landsberg girl that might add to the completion of the puzzle that confronted them.

He was pleased. The semen in the girl's vagina had come, no doubt, from Frank Rathlich. Then after he had left her, she had sneaked out to meet someone else, and he had killed her. But why? Because she had had sex with Rathlich? Or was there some other reason—a more profound reason not really connected with Rathlich at all? And most of all, who was it?

Macklin stopped suddenly and slapped his forehead with an open palm. Damn! It could be Rathlich's semen all right, but where did the Vaseline come from? Obviously, Rathlich had not used it, or was he lying about the Vaseline? No. The kid was sincere. He had to be. He was too naive to lie while under interrogation. Macklin shrugged, dug his hands deeper into his pockets, and walked on at a slower pace toward the administration building. Maybe, he had found out nothing at all significant. They'd just have to wait and see. But how long could they wait? If Jill's theory was correct, it had to be one of the others who had watched her with Rathlich. But which one was it?

12

The chimes in the tower of the administration building announced ten-thirty with one ringing note. In Falen Hall, the oldest of the girls' dormitories, a buzzer rang. A young girl clad only in a ratty old housecoat over panties and bra rolled over on a bed and flipped a switch near a speaker on the wall.

"Melba Stuart," she said into the intercom.

"Phone call for you, Miss Stuart." It was the dorm operator from the switchboard downstairs.

"I'll transfer it to phone number-one in your corridor."

Melba divested herself of the old robe and slipped on her newer terry robe and hurried down the hall. She lifted the receiver and said, "Hello."

"Mellie?" A soft masculine voice asked.

"Yes, is that you, Jerry?" The slip in using his first name was a reflection of her subconscious thoughts at that moment. A thrill rippled through her breast and spread down her arms. Her heart was beating like a triphammer.

"Mellie, are you busy now?"

"No, I was reading some things for English class, but

it's nothing pressing—why?'' A tinge of excitement was growing. It was the first time he had called her, and she could hardly wait to find out what he wanted. Oh, maybe at long last her dreams would come true!

"I'm snowed under with papers. You know the examinations from the other day. Would you mind giving me a hand in grading them? I'm at the office.''

"I'd be happy to. I'll be there in ten minutes. Okay?''

At last we'll be alone together, she thought, and at night too. Grading papers is just his way of getting me alone, I'll bet, she told herself. Her thoughts ran wild. She could already feel his strong arms cradling her, and the tender pressure of his lips gently caressing hers. She blushed slightly as she imagined his throbbing manhood pressing against her. Would he want to have sex with her? She hoped he would but she was also afraid because she didn't have the faintest idea of what she was supposed to do, how she was supposed to act in such a case. Oh, well, she'd just let nature take its course. He'd show her what to do. No need to worry. All she had to do was follow his lead. He'd be a good teacher. Everything was going to be just fine.

Back in her room she was all thumbs with nervous excitement. She managed to tug on a pair of jeans, pull a sweatshirt over her head and squeeze her feet into dirty sneakers. She paused in front of the mirror to add a little touch of lipstick, and to darken her eye shadow. She ran a brush through her hair, forcing herself to count twenty-five strokes. She felt rushed. She was overly anxious to be there in his arms, and, yet, she wanted to prolong the sweetness of being with him and so she dawdled. She thought about putting on a dress, but no, if Jerry loved her—wanted her—it wouldn't matter what she wore. She'd wear a dress for him at some other time.

She just had to go now. She couldn't wait any longer.

Hurrying across campus she saw a shadowy figure loping along a walk that intersected with the one she was following.

The shadow was a man, tall with broad shoulders and a muscular physique. She thought of Becky Mason propped over brick-studded concrete, and she thought of the man who had placed her there, and she thought of what that man may have done to her before he choked the life out of her. Her heart skipped a beat as the figure drew nearer. Once again her mind flashed to the picture of Becky Mason spread-eagled over those chunks of concrete in the ravine. She gasped as she felt her stomach muscles tighten in fear. She almost panicked and ran, then she recognized the man and breathed a sigh of relief.

"Melba Stuart, where are you going at this time of night?" He drew along beside her and wrapped a strong arm around her shoulders.

"Hi, Kevin. Where've you been?" She felt secure now. No killer would get her now, not while Kevin Rollins was with her. Kevin was Dr. Gulf's graduate assistant, and he kidded her nearly as much as Jerry did.

"I've been working out at the gym. But you didn't answer my question. A sexy chick like you shouldn't be wandering around alone on this campus with a sex-crazed killer on the loose." He gave her a snug squeeze. A hand moved up quickly to cup a breast. She allowed the hand to remain for one brief heartbeat, feeling herself respond to the gentle pressure, then she pushed his hand away, feeling flushed.

"Please, Kevin, don't do that!"

"Hey, Melba sweetie, what's the matter? You've got nice breasts—firm and not too large. Any guy would like to caress them, especially me. Not many things I like better'n stroking a lovely girl's—no, woman's —boobs. What's the matter, Melba, don't you like me?"

"Sure, I like you, Kevin. You're a great guy and a lot of fun to be with, but just 'cause I like you doesn't mean I want you to get fresh with me."

"Hey, I'm sorry. I didn't mean anything dirty by it. It was a loving gesture nothing more. I didn't know you'd get so uptight just because I copped a feel. Hey, after all, it is the twentieth century not the dark ages. There's nothing wrong with a little light petting between friends."

"Oh, Kevin! Please don't make fun of me. I just don't like for boys to get familiar with me that's all. I guess I'm just old fashioned but I don't like to be pawed."

"Okay, I'll behave." He slipped his arm around her shoulders again. Then suddenly he turned her and brought his lips down on hers, arching her back and squeezing her body close to his.

At first she fought the embrace and the kiss, keeping her lips firm and struggling in his arms. Then she surrendered to it, her passions rising and returned the kiss with heated fervor. She felt herself melt in his arms as if she were made of wax.

"Wow! You really know how to kiss! For an old fashioned girl—pardon the expression—you really know how to get a guy turned on. Boy!" He pulled her close for another hug and a brief, almost shy kiss, then held her tightly with his left arm and began to walk with her. "You didn't tell me where you are going."

She could see his mocking grin in the moonlight. "Well smarty, Dr. Gulf called and asked me to help him grade papers."

She felt triumphant and a tiny bit smug telling Kevin that Dr. Gulf had called her to help him even if it was late at night. She wondered if he thought this might be a clandestine meeting. Well, she didn't care. Let him think whatever he wanted to about her and Dr. Gulf. She halfway hoped that what he was thinking would come true, that is, if he was thinking that the meeting was, indeed, clandestine. That would show him.

"That's funny," Kevin said, hugging her still closer to him. "He didn't say anything about test papers to me. He did give a test this morning so he's got some to grade, and it's usually me that has to grade them, but he never mentioned them to me."

She could indeed see that Kevin was puzzled and she wanted to tell him it was because Jerry wanted to be alone with her. Then she forgot Kevin. She allowed her mind to wander to what might lie ahead for her in the science building. She'd let Jerry fondle her breasts if he wanted to or, for that matter, he could do anything he had a mind to do to her. She felt a rush of thrill-edged passion spread through her as she fantasized.

"Hey, you still there?"

"Huh? Oh, sure. My mind was wandering a little."

"It sure must have been. Were you thinking the same thing I was? I just can't figure why he didn't invite me over to grade those papers. Oh, well. I should be thankful for little favors. And thank you, Melba Stuart, for doing my work." He bowed royally in the moonlight.

"That's quite all right. It's my pleasure," Melba said as he locked his arm around her once more. "And the reason he didn't ask you is because he probably couldn't find you. You're always over at the gym lifting weights." Now that she had verbalized it what she had said made sense. She felt a quick moment of depression, then let her feelings soar again as she thought of Jerry waiting for her.

"What? Oh sure. You're probably right. He's been pretty busy all day—all week for that matter—on that research project of his. Probably didn't think of the test papers until tonight and I wasn't available."

They moved out onto the bridge.

"Hey, Kevin. Who's the chick?" A dark figure said as he passed them as they were about to step out onto the bridge.

"Hey, Carl. How's it going, man." Kevin said.

Melba huddled closer to Kevin. She had recognized Carl Watkins even before he had spoken to Kevin even if he hadn't recognized her. He had been rather persistent in asking her for dates of late, and she had been greatly disturbed at his vehement fits of anger that came each time she had refused him. She just didn't believe that Carl hadn't recognized her. He had to be pretending.

"Why did Carl do that?" Melba asked Kevin.

"Do what, sugar? What did he do? I didn't notice anything."

"You know. Pretend like he didn't know me?"

"Maybe he didn't recognize you. It is dark and there's only a little moonlight. Most likely he didn't take a good look."

"Nonsense! It's not that dark. He knew me all right! Kevin, I'm scared of him!"

"Hey, relax, sweetie. Carl's got a thing about white girls that's all." He stopped for a moment and leaned up against the railing. "He been bothering you?"

"Well, sort of. He's asked me for dates a few times."

"So you tell him to get lost if he pesters you again. He may get steamed a little but he'll get over it. Forget it. He'll just go after some other white girl. Carl's harmless."

"I'm not so sure of that. Didn't he date Becky Mason?"

"Yeah. I think so, but it doesn't mean anything." He wrapped his arm around her once more and started toward the science building. Melba held back.

"Hey. What's the matter? Hey, you aren't thinking that Carl killed Becky are you?"

"Well, why not. It's possible you know."

He frowned at her. "Sure, anything is possible. Becky whored around with a lot of guys, everybody knows that. So what if she dated Carl Watkins, that doesn't make him a killer."

"Maybe not. But he sure got mad when I told him I wouldn't go out with him. Suppose Becky went out with him and let him do whatever he wanted, then she suddenly wouldn't go out with him anymore. Do you think he would be capable of killing her then?"

"Well. . .when you put it that way, I suppose he could have done it, but I'm not convinced one-hundred percent yet. For that matter, Melba, it could be me. I played around with Becky a time or two. She was nothing but a big tease. She gave the come-on to every guy she ever met, and I'll bet on that."

"You didn't! You couldn't! Kevin, I always thought you were more of a gentleman than to fool around with a girl like Becky." She clapped a hand to her mouth. It was the first time she had admitted that Becky's reputation was anything but nice.

He laughed loudly. "Hey, Melba. Boy, you are naive. I love my wife, okay. With Becky it was just a mild flirtation. I didn't even really like her. She was too much of a whore for me. I just played her little game with her. There was no harm done to either her or me." He caught her hand and tugged. "Come on, I'll see that you get safely to the science building so Carl Watkins won't get you." He laughed a rollicking laugh that seemed to boom in the still night air.

Melba glanced back over her shoulder, but Watkins had vanished from sight. Shivering slightly, she couldn't shake the feeling that Watkins was watching them from the shadows somewhere.

They stopped at the door of the science building. "I'd go in and help with the papers, but my wife'd kill me. She's sure I'm carrying on with a student anyhow. Besides, Gulf probably wants to be alone with you." He winked knowingly.

She tried the door. It was locked. Kevin stepped past her and pulled at the door. "Damn," he muttered. "My key won't work in this door." He pulled a handful of keys from his pocket, inserted one into the lock, and turned but the lock wouldn't give. At least, it had appeared to Melba that he had tried the key but she couldn't be sure since he kept his hands shielded from her. "See, I told you it wouldn't work. Come on, we'll go around to the other side, it always works in that door."

He held her hand as he led her around the building to the other side. She could imagine men hiding in the shrubbery that grew along the side of the building just waiting to pounce on her. If it hadn't been for Kevin she'd have run screaming back to the dorm. She plodded along behind Kevin wanting desperately to run to the other side of the building. Oh, why did it take so long? She stopped, then uttered, "Ouch!" when her arm was jerked. Then she moved on. How had Jerry intended for her to get into the building? She didn't have a key. Had

113

he been watching for her? If he had then why hadn't he come and opened the door when she and Kevin tried it? Maybe he was embarrassed because Kevin was with her. Sure that was it, she told herself. He didn't want anyone to know that he and she would be alone in the science building.

They stopped at the doors, and Kevin slipped his arm around her once more as he searched for his keys. His hand moved up cautiously to cup her breast again. Melba spun in his arms and cracked his face with a stinging slap.

"Ow! Damnit, Melba! Why'd you do that. I just wanted to see if you are all real." A wide grin mocked her.

"I told you, Kevin, I don't like for boys to get fresh with me. Why can't you guys keep your hands to yourself. I don't like to be pawed!"

"I'm sorry. What the hell!"

He was mad. She could tell, and for a minute she felt sorry for slapping him.

"Hey, how about a little kiss?" He stepped toward her his arms outthrust.

"No! If you hadn't gotten so free with your hands, I might have let you kiss me, but not now!"

"Okay, Melba." He fished his keys out of his pocket, sorted through them, selected one and opened the door.

Melba blushing, rushed into the building and heard the door swish closed behind her. She stood there in the half light unsure of herself. She shouldn't have been so snotty. Kevin didn't mean any harm. It was just his way. She knew he flirted with all the pretty girls, and she felt sure he liked her and meant her no harm. She'd have to apologize—call him back and tell him she was sorry. Determined, she flung open the door and stepped out into the night again, careful to keep one hand on the door to stop it from closing. She saw Kevin disappearing around the corner, going in the opposite direction from the married student housing where he lived. She tried to call but she couldn't make her voice work. She stood forlornly, biting a knuckle with a tiny tear rising in the corner of her eye. He was gone.

She stood there for a long time, trying to get her emotions under control. Finally, she turned and entered the building and let the door close behind her. The corridor seemed so dim—much more so than usual. She peered around the corner. A rectangle of light projected from Gulf's office door. She sighed a long sigh of relief and felt her passions quickening again. She stepped into the restroom and ran a comb through her hair. She freshened her lipstick and wiped away a smeared smudge of mascara. Hesitantly, she re-entered the gloomy hall. She felt her anticipation mount as she tip-toed into Gulf's office.

A switch clicked throwing the room into near total darkness! A rough hand with a grip of steel clamped firmly over her mouth and shut off the scream building in her throat. She struggled uselessly. The grasp of the iron-like left arm held her securely. The unknown person held her tightly against them while a right hand fumbled at the fly of her jeans. The hand tore them open and stripped them down over her hips to bunch around her ankles. The person grasped her wispy panties and tugged. The elastic cut into the flesh of her back and thighs. Then the flimsy material gave and tore away leaving her naked from waist to ankles.

Panic seized her and she knew instantly that this was Becky Mason's killer that held her so cruelly. Struggling desperately, she bit down hard on the attacker's hand.

The person jerked the hand away with a yelp of pain. She was free! She emitted a shrieking wail and stumbled forward, trapped by the rumpled jeans. Steel fingers laced around her throat, choking off the scream in mid-pitch. The eerie half-light from the window began to swim before her eyes. Fear gripped her and she felt sad for in that instant she knew she was going to die. Her body grew numb. The pain in her throat was subdued by the constricting hands. She tried vainly to gasp—to fill her tortured lungs with precious air. Then the darkness grew deeper and blacker, then there was nothing anymore.

13

The phone on the scarred nightstand jangled incessantly. Pop Fischer jerked the blankets over his head, trying to shut out the irritating sound. It wouldn't stop—wouldn't leave him rest. Normally, he was an early riser, but the homicide had been on his mind last night and he had had trouble getting to sleep. Thus, this morning, he felt more tired than usual, and had no desire to get out of bed just yet.

The phone rang on despite his feeble attempts to ignore it—to shut it out of his conscious mind. Finally, he threw back the covers, sat up, ran a hand across his bald pate, and reached for the phone.

"Fischer, here," he said in an anger-tinged voice.

"Ira?" An equally gruff voice asked uncertainly.

"That's who you was callin' wasn't it," he said.

"Hold your skin together, Ira. Goddamnit, I don't like this any better'n you do, so let me give you this sonfabitchin' message will ya." He was half growling, half yelling.

"Yeah, Carmody," Pop growled. "Go ahead with it. What is it you got to say at this ungodly hour anyhow. And how come you ain't off duty yet? It's neigh on to eight-thirty. You should have been abed hours ago."

"Shit! Don't I know it. I give this city my time for all the good it does me. That bitch of a woman you hired didn't come in this mornin', so I stayed awhile longer than usual. Don't ask me why. I was just fixin' to leave when that bastard, Macklin, called. He said they'd found another girl chocked to death up to the college, and he wanted me to call you. So I'm callin' you. And you tell that bitch that her job's here at this damn desk same as mine and not jiggling around a murder scene!

"I'll do it, Carmody. Now, I ain't totally awake as yet, and anyhow I got in late last night, so you tell me once more what's goin' on in my city."

"All I know is what Macklin told me. He said we got another one—the Stuart girl, I think he said. Him and Riley is up to the college right now, and I think your broad-assed day watchman is up there too. Anyhow, I called Doc Spelchur, and his office said he'd be there as soon as they could find him. What else you need to know?"

"Where did they find the girl?"

"In the science building somewhere."

"Okay, Carmody," Pop said. "You can go home now and get your beauty sleep, and I'll be sure'n tell Jill her place is at that desk during the day and to be sure and relieve you on time from here on out." As he replaced the receiver, he chuckled to himself. Score one for Jill, he thought, and grinned widely.

He walked into the bathroom and looked in the mirror. A stubble of white whiskers covered his leathery cold cheeks. He held his shaving brush under the tap until it was saturated, then he twirled it around in a shaving mug creating frothy lather. This he brushed over his face. He stropped the worn straight razor on a leather

118

strap hanging from the lavatory, then scraped his whiskers off with quick, even strokes.

In the kitchen, after he'd dressed, he put the kettle on to boil. When he waited for the water to heat, he broke a raw egg into a glass of milk and drank it down. Next, he poured himself a cup of steaming-hot water, and stood sipping it over the sink. He never drank coffee nor tea, but he had a cup of hot water with every meal, and when others had a coffee break, he'd drink himself another cup of hot water. And if anyone had bothered to ask him why he drank hot water, which no one had done in years, he probably would have told them it was because the hot water wasn't a stimulant and it kept him feeling young chipper. No one was sure whether or not he believed it himslf, but it had once been a fond tale to tell.

Later, he eased the ancient Chevy into a vacant parking slot outside the science building, and trudged inside. Brockner, dressed in green work clothes, met him at the door.

"Hi ya, Pop. Yer lookin' feisty this mornin'."

"I ain't feelin' feisty, Brockner," he said. "What's awaitin' for me down the hall there?"

Brockner lost his pleasant look very quickly as it faded into a painful frown. "Another girl got herself killed. Last night sometime, I reckon. It's that one you was talking to out on the bridge, the other day."

"You mean the Stuart girl," Pop said.

"Yep, that's the one. She's half naked and colder'n a snake in a snow storm."

Pop pushed the cap over his forehead and scratched the fringe of graying hair.

"Them other cops said I was to wait for you and bring you along, sweetheart," Brockner said with a perfect Bogart lisp.

The old boxer led him along the corridor to the janitor's closet—really more of a room—which separated two class rooms. It was spacious for a storage room and clutterd with brooms, mops, pails, and containers of wax, soap powder, and paint. A table covered with a peeling oilcloth reposed against one wall. A battered, paint-chipped lunch bucket rested on the table.

Macklin, Jill, and Fenton Riley, one of the day deputies, were standing back away from the crumpled body of Melba Stuart. She lay in the middle of the floor, nude from the waist down. One leg was bent at the knee with the bottom of the foot resting against her other knee. Pop noted that her position was probably a contrived one and more than likely not the way she had lain when she had died. This one had the same marks of the looney that killed the other one. It had to be be the same person. Yet, there was something different about this one—something he couldn't quite place. Just a feeling he had about this one. Oh, well. It'd come to him in time. And time was a commodity he didn't have a great deal of anymore.

There had been a lot of confusion in his mind before this one. But now the killer had made a fatal mistake. He couldn't put his finger on it but he knew as well as he knew anything that he had him now. He no longer had any doubts but what he was going to get whomever it was that had killed the two girls.

"Where's Doc Spelchur?"

As if the county coroner had heard, he came through the door and gave Pop a reply first hand. "I'm right here," he said. He shook Macklin's hand, nodded at the others, and crouched to examine the body.

He was tall, at least six-four and had black wavy hair.

He wore a light blue pinstripe suit which obviously hadn't come off the rack. Momentarily, he glanced from his examination to smile at Jill. Jill blushed and turned to talk to Macklin, avoiding Spelchur's smiling countenance.

Pop watched Spelchur continue his examination of the body, then he glanced at Macklin and asked, "Who found her?"

"What was that?" Macklin asked as he turned from Jill to focus his full attention on Pop.

"Who found the girl?"

"Oh. Brockner," Macklin said, gesturing toward the old janitor.

"That right, Art?" Pop asked. "You found her?"

"Yep," Brockner said in a firm voice. "When I unlocked this morning, she was layin' right there just like you see her now. Now, that's a sight to greet you first thing in the morning, I'll tell ya."

"Hmm." Pop pushed the green cap foreward and scratched his head. Digging into his gaping sweater pocket he produced his charred pipe and from his hip pocket he brought forth a worn tabacco pouch. He busied himself for several minutes filling his pipe, tamping the tobacco tightly into place, and lighting it. After a while, puffing contentedly, he asked of no one in particular, "Where's her clothes?"

"No trace of them," Macklin said. "Just like the Mason girl, her clothes are gone—poof, disappeared."

"That right, Art? You didn't see her clothes?"

"Nope. Just like I said. That's the way she was when I opened up this morning. Half naked just as you see her now."

"What time did you open up?" Pop asked Brockner.

"It was a little after seven this morning. I come over

about six-thirty or seven every day. I was a little late this mornin' because I had to stop and get gas for my car. I get here early because I got to open all the classrooms before classes start at eight. After I open the rooms, I usually come over here and get me a pushbroom and a dustrag so I can tidy up a bit before the students start coming in. Let's see. I guess it was about seven-thirty or so by the time I got the classrooms opened. Then I come over here, and there she was.''

Pop continued to puff his pipe. He glanced over at Macklin and then at Riley. Macklin shrugged his shoulders and Riley looked at the ceiling. "Anybody else here when you come in this mornin'?''

'Well, let's see? Yep. There was Dr. Cagle and Dr. Worthington. They were in their offices which are both upstairs, but they come early every day.'' Brockner held out his hands palms up and shrugged his shoulders.

"What's your normal day like here?'' Pop asked, tamping the tobacco in his pipe with the butt of a pocket knife.

"Well, after I get things tidied up a bit—usually about ten or so—I go home. I come back in the afternoon, say about three most days. To keep up with the litter them students make, I got to keep at it while they're here. If I left it 'till they'd all gone, I'd never get it clean—not in one night's work anyhow. Then twixt four and seven I give her a real cleanin'. At seven we got night classes to go through with them students comin' in and makin' a mess all over again. So at ten, after most of them have gone, I give her another lick and a promise.''

"What time do you usually leave here at night,'' Pop asked.

"Oh, normally eleven-thirty or midnight. Sometimes

122

earlier—sometimes later. It depends,'' Brockner said warily.

"What time did you leave last night?" Pop asked as he pushed his still full but dead pipe into his sweater pocket.

"Let's see. . . It was earlier'n usual, cause I stripped down the floors on the first floor and put a new coat of wax on them last evenin'. I didn't touch the upstairs except for a sweepdown. I was gonna get them this morning before classes. All I did last night after night classes, which get out at nine-fifteen, was to buff up these floors here." He motioned toward the door with his hand. "I guess it must of been ten-fifteen or ten-twenty."

"Was anybody else here when you left," Pop asked.

"I didn't make no check to see who was still here. The only one I remember seein' before I left was Dr. Gulf. He was in his office workin' on those aerial pictures of his." Brockner cracked a grin. "Oh, yeah. There was some students in a chemistry lab upstairs but I don't know who they were."

Spelchur had finished his examination and stood, brushing the wrinkles out of his jacket and straightening his navy knit tie.

"Well, what's the verdict, Doc?" Pop asked, pressing his lower back with both hands and winching at the pain that was growing.

"There is very little doubt but what she was strangled. I would guess that whoever did it used his hands and choked her from behind." He ran a hand through his wavy hair. "You see the arrangement of bruises? Those were made by fingers clasped tightly around her throat." He glanced around at the expectant faces. "I suppose you want a full autopsy." It was more of a statement than a question issued as he picked at a piece of lint on his coatsleeve.

Pop nodded in the affirmative. "I want to be sure to know just how she died, and I want to know if she was done like the Mason girl."

Spelchur nodded and stepped to the door. He leaned into the hall and motioned. Two white-coated attendants appeared with a stretcher. They lowered it to floor level with a snap, hoisted the girl's body on the stretcher, covered the body with a sheet, popped the stretcher into a waist-high level, and wheeled it out again all in a very efficient, mechanical manner.

"Get me that information as soon as you can," Pop said.

"I will, Pop. I sure will. If my schedule's not too full, I'll have all the facts this evening at the latest."

"Good," Pop said. "We need to hurry along as fast as we kin on this. We can't afford for anymore gals to end up this way. He shook Spelchur's hand, and the doctor departed.

Pop turned back into the room and glanced at the other occupants. He was surprised that Jill had been quiet all this time. It wasn't like her not to get involved, but he was thankful for the silence. He noticed that Brockner was fidgeting.

"What's eatin' you, Art," he asked.

"Well—the girl ain't all I found!" It burst out like he had been forced to tell a secret.

"You found her clothes?" Pop asked.

"No, nothin' like that." He looked expectantly at Pop.

Pop looked around. The others were just as puzzled as he was, so whatever it was Brockner had found, he hadn't shared it with anyone as yet.

"Well, what was it, Art? What'd you find?"

"Come on, I'll show you." He led the way into the hall and knelt on the floor. "Kneel down," he said to Pop. "You can see 'em standin' up, but they show plainer down close."

"What show?" Pop asked exasperated. A pain was tightening the muscles on his neck at the base of his skull, and a spasm of pain was spreading across his lower back.

"Them," Brockner said, pointing at the floor. "You have to get the light just right."

Pop crouched down next to the janitor, ignoring the pain and studied the floor. He moved his head about, then he saw them. Two dull streaks in the otherwise glossy wax. The tracks led from the janitor's closet diagonally across the hall to Professor Jerry Gulf's office!"

"I figger whoever killed her dragged her across the hall from Dr. Gulf's office to this room. Them's heel marks or I ain't no janitor! And a newly waxed-floor is like a new car with me, I notice every little scratch."

Pop had to agree with the old boxer. It certainly appeared as if two rubber-soled shoes had been dragged across the floor, marring the wax. The body had been moved. That is why the position had looked contrived to him when he had first seen it. It had been moved and positioned in that obscene manner just like the Mason girl's body had been. But something was different! There was something here that hadn't been present with the other girl. He couldn't put his finger on what it was that was different but something didn't ring true about the whole scene. And it was something more than the fact that the body was the only half nude when the other girl had been totally naked.

Pop turned to Macklin. "Len, you stay close to the

office today. I got some things to do and I may need you quick-like. Riley, today you start a noon to midnight shift, and I want you to be close to this campus from four o'clock on. Collier'll be workin' a four to four and Ferguson will relieve you at midnight."

Riley grimaced but contained his anger.

"And, Jill." He looked at the girl. "From here on out, you relieve Carmody on time. God forbid that he should have to work a minute overtime."

Jill's face reddened.

Pop grinned broadly. "That poor ole one-legged man. I don't know why you two pick on him like you do."

Jill smiled just a trace, realizing that Pop was funning her but at the same time she knew he meant what he had said. He was actually trying to be nice to her. The old man had changed, and she was relieved even though she'd be back on the desk again and not working on the investigation—at least, not until he felt a need for her to go to work again

14

Pop was feeling a manic elation as he left the science building. He was anxious now—anxious to get on with it. For the first time he felt as if he had a grasp on the case; he knew what was needed of him now and what he had to do. The killer had finally made a big mistake; a mistake that would lead to his capture—or was it a she? Well, no matter now. Things would unfold as he went along.

The old man felt a mild ache of grief for the dead girl. It was unfortunate that she had to die, but because she did he now had a chance at the killer. The first murder had been spontaneous. Of course, it was probably planned to a certain degree, he didn't doubt that, but in essence it was mostly spontaneous. And a spontaneous crime was a difficult one to solve. Had the murderer stopped with the first girl, he felt reasonably sure that he would never have brought him to justice.

Pop chucked to himself. Jill was just enough of a woman's libber to frown on his use of the masculine in identifying the unknown killer in his thought until he had a positive identification. He wasn't positive yet. It could still be any one of his suspects, and what he had to find was the relationship of the killer with the two girls. That much was obvious. The killer had a definite relationship with both girls. The second homicide was well planned and well executed and for a different motive than the first. The second was an attempted cover-up for the first and that was where the murderer had made his big mistake.

Pop parked the old Chevy in front of a row of brick apartments. There were eight units to a complex, each two units separated by a breezeway which also served as a stairwell to the second story apartments.

A small girl and boy went racing by on the sidewalk in front of the apartments. The boy was earnestly pumping the pedals of a Big Wheel and pulling a little girl in a wagon. The little girl was clutching the sides of the wagon in a half-terrified frenzy.

Pop found the door he sought which opened off a breezeway on one of the middle, downstairs apartments. He punched a button and heard a bell's muffled ring somewhere inside the apartment.

Pop looked back at the painted, wooden door as it swung open. A slender woman, pale face devoid of make-up and hair in curlers, stood behind the screen door which separated them. The look on the girl's pretty face was one of annoyance, and Pop realized just how out of place he must look ringing the door bell in the college's student-housing complex.

Pop fumbled a wallet out of his hip pocket and opened it so the woman could see the silver star pinned to a flap.

"Ira Fischer, Chief Constable here in the Cape," he said in a matter of fact voice. "Are you Mrs. Rollins—Mrs. Kevin Rollins?"

"Yes, I'm Mrs. Rollins. Is there something wrong? Is

it Kevin? He's not hurt is he?''

"No, ma'am." He answered all of her question at once. "Is your husband to home?"

"No," she said hesitantly. "No, Kevin has gone to class. Why do you ask? Has. . .has he done something wrong?"

"No, ma'ma. As far as I know, yer husband is fine. Could I ask you a few questions?"

"Yes. I guess so. What about? Is Kevin involved in something unlawful?"

"Can't rightly say for sure, ma'am. Er. . .do you mind if I come inside? I feel sort of self conscious standin' here gabbin' with you through the screen."

"Oh, I'm sorry. Please come in," she said, clutching the pink robe close about her throat and swinging the screen door wide.

Pop stepped inside. The apartment was simple in its arrangement. An L-shaped room served as a living room and a kitchen. Another room, which would have completed a cube was walled off with a door leading to its interior. A bathroom, Pop guessed. Beyond it on the back wall were two more doors. The bedrooms, Pop surmised.

"Won't you have a seat?" she asked, swinging her arm along the room that ran the full length of the apartment. It was furnished with tough-looking, vinyl-covered furniture, and was, no doubt, the same in every apartment in the complex.

The women was pretty enough all right, but she looked so washed out. She didn't have a bit of color atall. What it did was make her look fragile, like she'd break with the tinyest squeeze.

Seeing her, he wondered what Rollins looked like. Images of skinny fellows or fat ones ran through his mind. A guy with thick-lensed glasses perced on a long pointed nose, no doubt. A man with a real intelligent look about him. Pop frowned. The image that Mrs. Rollins created in his mind sure didn't fit his idea of a geology major. No, sir. A geologist had to be a muscular tough guy, capable of withstanding the rigors of living and working in the wilds. That image also fit better the image they had gleaned from the interrogations they had held so far. Yep. A handsome muscular man it had to be, despite the images of her husband that Mrs. Rollins seemed to generate in his mind.

Pop planted his two hands on the chair arms and lowered himself slowly into one of the two vinyl chairs. he turned his head. The woman was standing just out of his reach, looking at him like she was still wondering why he was here.

"Could I get you a cup of coffee?"

He scratched a cheek. "Uh. . .no, thankee, ma'am. I never touch the stuff. But. . .er. . .if you don't mind, I'll have a cup of hot water though."

"Hot water!" the woman said in disbelief. "Oh, well whatever you want." She shook her head and turned toward the kitchen.

"Yes, ma'am. I like a hot drink now and again, but I don't care for the effects of coffee and tea. They stir up nerves somethin' fierce. Yep, hot water does me just fine."

She returned from the kitchen with a cup of hot water for him and coffee for herself. She handed him the water and sat down across from him on the couch.

He sipped the hot liquid and sighed like an alocholic taking his first drink of the day. Mrs. Rollins was tucking the skirt of her robe primly around her legs, then she carefully crossed her legs.

"Now, what is it you wanted to ask me? I don't mind telling you that you have me puzzled."

He nodded as he sipped more water. "Your husband's Professor Gulf's assistant now ain't he?"

"Yes. He works for Dr. Gulf, but I don't understand," she said, clutching the front of her pink robe. "Is Kevin in some sort of trouble? And I don't see what Jerry Gulf has to do with this anyhow."

"Mebbe, he's involved—your husband that is. I don't rightly know yet. He have access to the professor's office?" He pushed a fist into a gaping sweater pocket and, with his other hand, he took a tighter hold on the cup handle.

"Yes, Kevin has a key to Dr. Gulf's office. Actually, he shares an office with Dr. Gulf. At least, the offices have a common entrance. It's just the typical thing for graduate assistants." She brushed a lock of hair that had become disengaged from a curler out of her eyes. "Something has happened hasn't it? Is Kevin all right?" Her robe gaped, exposing a frilly pink nightgown. Her ample breasts were heaving against the thin frabric. She hurriedly gathered the front together again. Her face was stained a light crimson. Pop looked away.

A moment later he smiled at the woman's embarrassment. The color does her fine, he thought. Yep. A little color in her cheeks and she's a downright purty gal. He said, "He's fine, ma'am, as fer as I know, just fine."

Mrs. Rollins looked perplexed, and there was a troubled frown worrying her blue eyes.

"What time did your husband get home last night?" he asked and drained the last of the hot water from his cup.

The woman frowned a deeper frown as if she were having trouble sorting out the answer. "Just about midnight, I think. Yes. I remember it well now. I was kinda miffed about him being so late, and I was in bed but not asleep. I recall the chimes ringing twelve just after he came in." She frowned again which seemed to increase the paleness of her face. "Why do you ask? Has it something to do with Dr. Gulf?"

Pop took a deep breath and exhaled audibly. He reached a hand into his shirt pocket and grasp a pipe and started to pull it out. He glanced around the room and back at Mrs. Rollins. The hand froze, and he dropped the pipe back into place gently.

"Girl was killed up to the college last night. Just a routine check, that's all."

"A girl killed!" Her face betrayed her shocked reaction. "Surely, you can't seriously think that Kevin had anything to do with a murder—do you?"

"Can't rightly say, ma'am." Pop shrugged his shoulders and again looked around the room, avoiding her gaze. "He knew the girl, and his whereabouts last night are in question—" He shrugged his shoulders again. "So, yes, ma'am, he's a suspect."

"Oh, my God!" She broke into sobs and buried her face in her hands.

Pop levered himself out of the chair. He wasn't sure what he should do, so he stood, holding the cup in his right hand. After a while the woman looked up at him, tears streaming down her face, a unspoken plea resting on her lips but obvious in her facial expression.

"Mrs. Rollins. I wish I could say different but yer husband is a suspect, at least, until we know different. But the changes that he had anything to do with the homicide are probably not so good. I don't want you to get yerself all riled up over nothin'."

The color was back in her cheeks, and her robe was

gaping open ignored. She evidently didn't care anymore that she was more exposed than covered. Pop could see that her emotions were mixed now. She was angry that her husband had let himself get in a position where he could be suspected of murder and she was also worried about him. He was glad at that moment that he wasn't Kevin Rollins because he could see she was meaning to take him to task when he got home. He handed her the cup which she took automatically, twisting her face into a firm, angry mask. She didn't believe it for one minute that her husband was capable of murder.

"I told him not to keep playing around with those college coeds. He said he had to be nice to them because he was a graduate assistant and that's something like a teacher. But I knew he was being more than nice to them, and I warned him. Damn him!"

Pop shoved the rumpled cap back on his head and headed for the door.

"Mr. Fischer!"

"Yes, ma'am?" he said, turning at the door.

"If you see Kevin, you tell him I want to see him at home as soon as possible."

"I'll do that, ma'am," he said and took his leave.

15

Pop shambled down the walk to his old Chevy. He look-ed about him but there was no sign of the small children who had been playing here just a short time ago. It was almost silent with only the trilling of a bird somewhere breaking the quiet.

He opened the car door and lowered himself onto the seat, swinging his tired old legs beneath the wheel. The car started quicky when he turned the key, and the engine purred smoothly as he shifted the car into gear and pulled away from the curb.

He felt sorry for the young woman and he had just left behind. There was nothing he could do to help her, and she appeared to be fighting a losing battle, and she was doing more to help her adversary then she knew. And she wasn't helping herself with her tactics. Her husband was fooling around with young coeds. She had implied as much. That didn't make him a murderer but it did cause Pop's interest in him to be sharpened a bit. But he wouldn't give it much thought until something more definite pointed in that direction.

Right now his thoughts turned to the woman again and her immediate problem. He pitied her not just because of her husband's wanderings but because of herself. He had seen many, many women like her over the many years that spanned his adult life. They seemed to gain a strong sense of security and developed a strong attitude of proprietorship toward their husbands once that small band of gold was placed on their fingers. They took the vows that said "forever until death do us part" to heart and forgot that both partners had to contribute to a marriage to make it work. They were sincere, perhaps, in the course they chose and maybe never knew what they were doing. They permitted themselves to become slovenly and overweight; they nagged their men endlessly, then wondered why they strayed. They couldn't see how their constant disheveled appearance had anything to do with driving their men into the arms of other women.

They did nothing to retain the character that had attracted the men they married in the first place. The day was spent in a worn robe, hair in curlers, face devoid of make up, then wondered why their husbands were always chasing other women.

Mrs. Rollins was a case in point. She was still a beautiful woman with a pretty face and a comely shape, and if she took care of herself like she had done when they were dating, he would be willing to bet that her husband wouldn't always be off chasing some coed. He felt very positive about that, and if her husband had been at home with her last night, or if they had been out together having a good time, he wouldn't be a suspect in a homicide. Of course, there was the possibility that he might just be the killer they were seeking. Of course, if this were true he couldn't blame Mrs. Rollins now could he?

Smiling, he thought of Shirley. She had never been

like that. She had taken care of her man and had seen to it that his every whim had been satisfied. She had tried to be pleasing to him at all times. She always had been refreshing, especially when he had come home from work in the evening. And she had worn dresses always. He could never remember seeing her in pants, and he had liked that. To him a woman was much more fetching, much more feminine in a skirt, and he respected them more for that. Oh, he accepted the excuse that pants were more comfortable. He chuckled. Whatever happened to the women of his youth? Women were women then and not striving so hard to be like men. Ah, for the good old days.

Then, as it always did when he thought of Shirley, the cancer crept into his mind. That ravaging disease that had stolen his love; taken the most cherished part of his life; leaving him a lonely and broken old man who spent his time tinkering with an old car and being a policeman.

He pulled the aged Chevy over against the yellow curb, ignoring the no parking sign. He climbed laboriously out of the car, and walked slowly across the walk and into the student union building. He was gambling that he would find Kevin Rollins inside. And what he had learned about Rollins so far in his investigation of the case led him to believe that Rollins was the type to spend his time in the campus social center, more than likely conversing with a coed or even several coeds. Of course, if he were wrong in his assessment of Rollins, or if he happened to be in class, then he wouldn't find him here.

He realized he didn't know who he was looking for and he would have to ask someone or several someones until he found a person that knew who Kevin Rollins is, then have that person point him out. That is, if he were here.

Now who would most likely be acquainted with Kevin Rollins? he asked himself. If what he had heard about the man thus far was typical, then the best person to ask would be a girl. He looked around. A girl in tight jeans and a floppy shirt was bending over a cigaret machine which rested against the wall to his right, studying the various brand names.

"Excuse me, miss," he said.

"Yes?" Her eyes flicked over him from head to foot and the smile faded.

"Do you by any chance know Kevin Rollins?"

"Kevin Rollins? Oh, gee, yeah." She turned toward the mass of students in the dining area and squinted her eyes as she peered out over the room. Presently, she pointed over toward the center of the congregation and said, "That's him over there in the middle. See, the good-lookin' blond guy talking to the dark-haired girl."

He followed the girl's pointing finger and found the blond fellow she had mentioned.

"Thanks," he said.

"Don't mention it," she said.

He studied Rollins for a moment. He was indeed good looking, even handsome. He had a husky, muscular build and a pretty face, topped off by platinum-blond, wavy hair. He was slouched in his chair, but Pop guessed that he would stand an inch or two over six feet.

Pop walked on down the aisle to a door which led to the food-dispensing area. He pushed through the door and stopped at a coffee urn with three spigots with clear tubes rising above them. He took a styrofoam cup from a stack and filled it from the spigot which had a clear liquid in its tube. Then he moved over to the cashier.

"Would you like a tea bag, sir?" A middle-aged woman asked. She wore her gray-speckled hair combed severely back into a neat bun at the back of her head. She was wearing a red smock.

"Nope. Just the hot water," he said.

"Just hot water? No coffee? No tea? Just hot water?"

"Yep."

"Well! This is highly unusual. I'll. . .I'll just have to charge you a nickel for the cup. That's our policy."

"Okay by me," Pop said and pulled a handful of change from his pocket and carefully counted out five pennies.

Out in the dining area once more, he checked to see if Rollins was still at the table. He was. Pop threaded his way among the students to Rollins's table.

"Mind if I join you?" he asked.

Rollins looked him over carefully and frowned. The dark-haired girl gave him scant attention. It was obvious that Rollins was the focus of her interest.

"Yes, I mind," Rollins said. "Janice and I are having a private conversation, so you'll have to find another table, old man." Rollins was obviously perturbed.

Pop set his cup on the table and pulled out his wallet. "I think not," he said as he flashed his badge. "Mind if we talk private?"

Rollins appeared dumbfounded and just stared at Pop for several seconds. Then he said, "Well, I guess not." Turning to the girl, he said, "Janice, will you excuse me?"

"Why not," the dark-haired girl said with a hurt look. "See you around, love." She walked away, hips swinging.

"Pretty girl," Pop said, looking at the gold band on Rollins's left hand.

"Yeah. What'd you want to see me about?"

Pop took his time in answering. He dug out his old pipe, and busied himself lighting it. "Where was you last night?"

"Me?" Rollins looked surprised. "Hey, what's going on here? What do my whereabouts last night have to do with anything?"

"In due time, Rollins, in due time. First, I want an answer to my question. Where were you last night?"

"Starting when? I'm a busy guy with school and all."

Pop puffed on his pipe and sipped some of the hot water. "Let's say after supper. Where'd you go and what did you do after supper last night?"

Rollins shrugged his massive shoulders. "Hey, let's see. After supper I went out to the driving range and hit a bucket of balls. I've got to keep my golf game smooth. Then I went over to the field house and worked on the weights. I lift weights every day without fail. After that I went home." He slowly tore his styrofoam coffee cup into small pieces.

"What's this all about anyway?"

"What time'd you leave the field house?" Pop asked around his pipe stem.

A girl tugged playfully at Rollins's long hair as she walked past the table. Rollins ignored her, and she turned with a frown on her face. She looked at the back of his head for a moment, saw Pop and formed a big O with her lips. Then she wound her way over to a table occupied by several hulking brutes that Pop assumed were football players and took a seat. Pop turned his attention back to Rollins.

Rollins brow furrowed. "Let's see. I quit on the

139

weight about ten—took a shower." He looked up at the ceiling. "I guess it must have been about ten-thirty."

A girl dropped a quarter into the juke box, pushed some buttons and loud, raucous music blared through the room.

Pop winced at the loud noise. "You went home then, you say?"

"Yeah, that's right. Why?" He chewed the end of a plastic spoon.

"See anybody on the way?"

Rollins wrinkled his brow, then grinned. "Yes, as a matter of fact, I did. I ran into Melba Stuart—a geology student. I walked her over to the science building where my car was parked. Oh, yeah, we passed Carl Watkins on the bridge." He smiled smugly.

Pop tapped his pipe in the ashtray and finished his cup of water. "This took place about ten-thirty, right?"

Rollins nodded.

"What time did you get home then?"

Rollins shrugged his shoulders and turned his shoulders and turned his hands, palms upward. "Oh, ten—fifteen minutes later. About a quarter to eleven. Why?" He was still grinning.

"Hmm," Pop said, shoving his cap forward over his forehead and scratching his head. "How come your wife tells me it was midnight when you come in? Said you arrived as the college chimes rang."

Rollins blanched. His hands shook and his eyes rounded. "Oh, yeah. I forgot. I had a flat."

"Took you over an hour to change a flat?" Pop applied a kitchen match to his now dead pipe. Another rock tune blared from the juke box just as noisy as the first.

Rollins threw out his hands, palms up. "I didn't have

a spare. I had to roll it all the way down to the Texaco service on Harrison and Elm. That's the only one that stays open all night.''

"Hmm," Pop muttered. "Melba Stuart was strangled in the science building last night." He said it in a way, hoping to get maximum shock from Rollins.

Rollins stared wide-eyed, mouth agape. The reaction seemed to Pop to be authentic enough.

"Melba Stuart? Why, I can't believe that. Why—"

"You were saying, Rollins," Pop said.

"Nothing. Nothing. I wasn't going to say nothing."

"You said you were with her last night after you finished lifting them weights. That'd be about ten-thirty now wouldn't it?"

"Okay. Yeah. I met her outside the dorm. I just happened to run into her on my way over to the science building to get my car. I walked her over there and saw to it that she got safely into the science building, then I went on my way."

Pop wondered if Rollins was trying to be cagy in admitting that he had been with Melba Stuart shortly before her death.

"Hmm," he said. "Why was she going to the science building at that time of night?"

Rollins chuckled. "She said that Jerry. . .er, Dr. Gulf had called her and asked her to come over and help him grade papers." He was grinning mysteriously now.

"Grade papers? I figgered that was graduate student work. How come you wasn't doin' the gradin'?"

"Well, normally it is my job to grade papers, but for some reason he didn't call me. He called Melba instead."

"He called Melba?"

"That's right. She said he had called her just a few

minutes before I ran into her. She said that he had called her and asked her to come over to the science building and help him grade papers."

"Why'd he do a thing like that? Ain't it a bit unusual?"

"Yeah, it was unusual. Oh, hell. I might as well say it and get it out in the open. He was sweet on her. It was his way of getting her alone without raising the suspicions of the college administration."

"You know this for a fact do you?"

"I know Jerry Gulf. He's somewhat of a lecher. Yes, I am sure that he was very strongly attracted to her."

"Enough so he'd kill her?"

"She was. . .she was a favorite student of his, and if she threatened to expose his. . .if she. . .oh, hell. I don't know."

"Hmm," Pop said.

"Look, I don't know if he'd kill her but he'd go to bed with her if he had the chance. That much I'm sure of."

"Hmm," Pop said. "How about Becky Mason? He sweet on her too, was he?"

"Oh, now wait a minute. You're trying to get me to point the finger at Jerry. I'm not going to do that."

You've already pointed the finger at him, Pop wanted to say. Instead, he said, "I see." He toyed with his styrofoam cup. "How'd he treat the Stuart girl?"

"Well, he teased her a lot. He only teases those he likes. And he'd call her into his office frequently for discussions, usually about the class."

"Could he have fooled with her at those times?"

"I suppose. All he had to do was close the door, and I guess he could do whatever he pleased."

"Did he close the door?"

Rollins looked perplexed. "On some occasions. No. On most occasions. But I don't know what they were doing in there."

"How about the Mason girl? He tease her?"

"Some. But not nearly as much as the Stuart. . .not as much as Melba."

"He call her into his office to talk?"

"Let's see. Yes. Yes, he did."

"He close the door?"

"I don't know. I just can't remember. Let it drop will you?"

"Hmm," Pop said. He emptied his pipe in the ashtray. "Yer office is next to Gulf's. Think hard. Did he close the door when he had the Mason girl in there?"

"Oh, damn you!" He was shouting now and students all around the table were turning and staring. More quietly he said, "Yes, he closed the door. Practically with every student—female anyway—he closed the door. Now are you satisfied?"

Pop grinned. "I'll keep in touch. I know I'll want to talk to you agian soon." He shuffled off ignoring the stares of the students that had witnessed Rollins's vociferous answer.

16

Sherrill Olson scrawled his name at the bottom of a document, then tugged his ear lobe as he surveyed a pile of reports lying on his desk. He sighed, selected the top report, the leaned back in his comfortable office chair to read. A long day lay ahead of him and most of it was going to be spent in this office.

He was halfway through the first page of the report when his intercom buzzed. He reached over to flick the switch to answer when the door burst open and a raging Claude Dale bulled his way into the room. Sherry, his secretary, stood in back of him her arms extended downward in a helpless gesture.

"Shirrell, I warned you. Now, you've let things go too far. We have another dead girl on our hands, and the town is not going to stand for it. I want Ira Fischer out of office now! And, believe me, I mean now!"

"Relax, Claude, before you have a coronary. We had an agreement or don't you remember. I've still got nearly twelve hours."

"Shirrell, your time has run out as of now. I told you twenty-four hours, providing we didn't have another butchered coed. Now, we have one, and I am calling my ultimatum!"

"Claude! Calm down. The girl was strangled just as the other one was. And Spelchur doesn't think she was forcefully raped. We're working on it, and I hope to have an arrest within the day."

"That's a small consolation. So she wasn't raped. She's dead just the same isn't she?"

Dale took a seat, crossed his legs, and locked his hands together, fingers intertwined. "Just what are you doing, Shirrell? Have you got the killer identified from that morass of suspects that seems to be bothering Fischer? This police department is the most impotent of any in this country. There is no scientific basis to it at all. Why we don't even have a fingerprint kit let alone any sort of a forensic lab. I guess whatever Spelchur can contribute in that area is as close as we can come to a lab. Any arrest that you can manage will come from slipshod happenstance and not from scientific police investigation."

Olson tapped a pencil on his desk. Inside he could feel his emotions boiling. Right now he would feel perfectly justified to grab Claude Dale's throat in his two hands and choke the life out of him. His hands were itching to do just that. Instead, he pushed his bubbling emotions to a back burner and composed himself.

"Claude, this department is not designed to handle a murder case. I won't deny that. But then we don't have a murder case in a town this size that often. We have to gear ourselves for the type of crime we encounter most frequently. And that is not homicide. I feel perfectly confident that Pop can handle this homicide, and I am sure he will have a suspect incarcerated in due time. We are taking every precaution to insure that no more young ladies are molested on the campus. So, please, Claude, give us just a little time."

145

"Sorry, Sherrill. I've given you all the time that can be afforded. My demands will be met! I want Fischer relieved of duty this very instant or I will make you sorry you ever appointed the old man to the job in the first place!"

Dale leaped to his feet and shook a pointed index finger in Olson's face. "It's no good, Shirrell. I've wasted enough time with you. I thought you could see the seriousness of the situation. Obviously, you can't or you refuse to recognize it. Thus, I've got to act. You leave me no choice."

"Claude, what will be accomplished by taking Pop off the case at this point. He is competent no matter what you think. And replacing him gains us nothing."

"Competent? That old fool is so senile that he's. . . he's. . .not sure what's going on." Dale was sputtering. His fury was on the verge of consuming him.

"I'm sorry, Claude. I see no advantage in replacing Pop at this point in the investigation. Do what you feel you have to do and get it over with. I won't try to stop you. Have at it, damn you!"

Dale's face was a bright scarlet, and he was gurgling as he tried to talk. "I've given you your last chance, Shirrell Olson. Now, I'll make you regret your actions. You'll rue this day until the day you die." He gave one threatening shake of his balled fist and stormed out of the door, slamming it with a thudding boom!

Olsen sat down at his desk once more and tried to relax. His anger was long in subsiding, and he was still shaking as he picked up the phone and dialed a number.

He could hear the ringing through the receiver. Then a soft female voice said, "Police headquarters. Officer Reardon speaking. May I help you?"

"Miss Reardon. This is Mayor Olson. Is Pop around?"

"No, sir. He's still up at the campus. He said he had some investigating to do. Is there anything that I can do?"

"Thank you, no, Miss Reardon. Can you contact him for me?"

"No, sir. Pop doesn't have a radio in his car. I'm not even sure where he is at the moment. I guess I can send someone to find him if you like."

"That will be fine. Tell him to get in touch with me at his earliest convenience. It's very important."

"Yes, sir. I'll do that right away."

Well, the wheels were in motion, he thought. There was going to be hell to pay if Pop wasn't far along enough to move quickly to make an arrest. Olson wasn't sure what he was going to do at this point. He hated to give in to Claude Dale, but the man had a point. He just couldn't see replacing Pop in favor of Macklin. Just what was that supposed to accomplish other than easing Dale's anger and assuaging his ego? Well, he'd talk to Pop and then make up his mind. Maybe it would best to let Pop go. Maybe it was time for a change. Pop had been on the force for over fifty years, that he knew of. Exactly how long he couldn't say although he could find it in the files if he really needed to know. He hated to have to act but he just didn't know what else he could do. Maybe it was for the best. He sighed again and leaned back in his chair.

17

Pop started his old Chevy. He had two more calls he wanted to make today. Sitting back, while the engine purred languidly, he reflected on the whole situation. He had a strong feeling that Rollins was lying. Should he let it go at that? Just play his hunch? No, he'd better check out the kid's story. When a man and his wife can't agree on a story something is wrong. He backed the Chevy out and nosed it toward the street. Rollins was lying and he didn't know why unless he was responsible for the death of the Stuart girl. Rollins was a campus playboy. That was fact but just how serious his picadillos were was questionable. It was beginning to look like he'd had opportunity and possibly even a motive. If he'd been stringing the girls along, he could imagine what could happen if there was a threat to reveal all to his wife. It all depended on how much Rollins really loved his wife and whether or not he would kill to preserve it.

They were questions Pop couldn't answer. But they kept filling his head and each time one filtered through his mind, it seemed more reasonable. Was the pressure getting to him? Was he really worried about Shirrell

Olson enough to effect an arrest just to placate Claude Dale? No. Dammit! He wasn't going to act until he was sure and he certainly wasn't sure of Kevin Rollins.

He swung the Chevy into the Texaco station and rolled to a stop near the building. An eager-looking lad came over to lean on the door.

"Can I help you, sir?"

Pop looked up at him. He had tousled brown hair stuffed under a greasy gray hat with a Texaco emblem on the front.

"Nope," Pop said. "I want to talk to Ned Chambers."

"Ah. Mr. Chambers is inside. In his office."

A bell rang, and a car rolled up to the pumps. The boy adjusted his cap and trotted over toward the new customer.

Pop toiled his way out of the car and walked slowly toward the building. He walked through an inner door and into the service area. A car was hoisted on the rack and a man was busy underneath. Tires of various sizes lined the back wall nearly to the ceiling. A door to his right opened through the cinder block wall and into a cramped office. A chubby-looking man with wiry, black hair was seated at a desk thumbing through a stack of charge tickets with his left hand and punching a calculator with his right.

"Howdy, Ned," Pop said.

The man looked up, punched the calculator once more and ran a grease-stained hand under his nose.

"Hello, Pop. What brings you out this way. Don't tell me. The guy who killed that college girl filled his tank here." The man laughed, slapping his knee.

"Mebbe. But that ain't why I'm here. Need to know if a young feller got a flat tire fixed in here last night."

Chambers scratched his wiry hair just behind the ear.

"Can't say that we did." He looked puzzled. "What time'd he bring it in? Can you tell me about time it was?"

"Close enough, I reckon. It'd have been somewhere around eleven, to eleven-thirty, mebbe even eleven-forty-five."

"I wasn't here then," Chambers said. "I got two or three college boys that work the night shift. I don't feel likely that they'd change a tire though. They don't want to do any more than pump gas and pour oil. Of course, if somebody brought a tire in for fixing, I don't suppose they'd turn them down."

He stood up and ran a finger over a calendar-like schedule taped to the wall above his desk. "That'd be Sonny Blake. Let's see—" He fumbled for a small book in his middle desk drawer and flipped the pages until he found the listing he wanted. Still looking at the book, he pulled the desk phone over to him and dialed, holding the receiver in his dialing hand. The phone rang a long time. He kept looking at Pop with an apologetic look on his face. Finally, he said, "Hello. Hello. I want to talk to Sonny Blake. Is he in. Yeah, I'll hold."

Several minutes went by. Then suddenly he said, "Sonny?" A pause. "This is Chambers. Did you have a tire to fix, say about eleven to eleven-thirty?"

He listened awhile longer, said, "Thanks," into the phone and hung up. He turned to Pop. "Sorry, but Sonny says that there wasn't anybody brought in a tire to fix last night."

Pop scowled, twisted his lips into a grimace, nodded his head and shuffled out of the garage toward his car.

"Thanks, Ned," he called back over his shoulder to Chambers who had followed him outside.

150

It was nearly noon when Pop arrived at the science building. He was still confused in his own mind. Something was tugging at him and he couldn't identify it. Jerry Gulf was drawing him back for another question and answer session. There was something about Gulf that drew him—something about the man that didn't set right at all.

Gulf was still in his office, apparently working diligently. Before him lay a long narrow paper tape about four inches wide. On the tape were wriggling lines which reminded Pop of the electrocardiogram he took each year at his physical examination necessary for him to keep his job.

Gulf looked up from his intent scrutiny of the long tape.

"Good morning, Mr. Fischer. It is still morning isn't it?"

Pop eyed him suspiciously. "Yep. It's still mornin' but just barely. What's that there you're studyin' so hard?"

"This?" Gulf said. "This is an electric log. It tells me which rock formations are permeable and whether or not they are holding any fluid and what density that fluid is. An electric log is very essential to finding petroleum."

"I see," Pop said, pushing his cap over his forehead and scratching his head behind his ear.

"I hear you had another murder last night," Gulf said.

"Exactly what did you hear?"

"Just a rumor that you and your staff were here this morning early, and that another body was carried out."

"It's more'n rumor. There was another girl killed here last night. Anyhow, I think she was killed here. It's possible, of course, that she was killed elsewhere and brought here, but I doubt it." Pop screwed up his face in thought. Then he ambled over to lean against the drafting table at the back of the room.

"Where was you last night, Professor Gulf?"

"Me? You can't possibly think I did it, can you?" He shrugged his shoulders. "Well, maybe you can think that after all." He smiled and placed his hands on his hips and looked Pop in the eye.

"I was at home. As a matter of fact I turned in right after dinner with a good book and a bottle of Chivas Regal. I tied on a good one. Staring at these photos and these logs gets to one after a while. I find getting a little drunk helps me unwind."

"Anybody verify that for you?"

"You forget, Mr. Fischer, I am a bachelor. I live alone." He frowned. "I really am a suspect is that it? Who am I supposed to have killed?"

Pop ignored the question. "You by any chance have a young coed visiting with you last night?"

"Hell no!" he shouted. "Look, I don't have to stand here and take this from you. If you have questions, ask them. But don't insinuate that I fool around with the coeds on this campus. Is that clear?"

Pop studied him for a moment. "No need to get all riled up about it I just asked a simple question. I got to know all the facts and I got to know'em fast. We can't afford to get any more gals killed. So I aim to wrap this caper up as fast as I can. And, yes, you are a suspect—a strong suspect. So, you just answer my questions and never mind what you think I might be insinuatin'. It don't make no difference noway."

"All right. I'll try and keep my temper controlled. But at least you could tell me who it is I'm supposed to have killed."

152

Pop stared at him with narrowed eyes. "The Stuart girl," he said calmly.

"Mellie!" The shock looked genuine. "My God! You can't mean that—not Mellie!" He shook his head and rubbed a hand across his eyes. "You think I killed her don't you? You're crazy, simply crazy. I liked that girl very much—maybe too much. She was fun. I enjoyed having her in class. She made some rather useless days seem worthwhile for me. Why, I think I could even have. . .well, even have fallen in love with her if she hadn't been a student." A tear showed at the corner of his eye. "Oh, hell, I guess maybe I was in love with her! I couldn't have killed her—not Mellie."

"Not even if she threatened to go to the dean?"

"The dean? What does he have to do with this?" He was frowning.

Was it possible Gulf didn't understand what he had meant when he had said she might go to the dean?

"Wait a minute. I see what you're driving at. You think I was involved with her and that she threatened to blackmail me with threats of going to the dean and revealing our supposed relationship." He laughed loudly and folded his arms across his chest. Pop waited.

"It sounds like a good motive but there's no truth in it." He turned away, then suddenly swung back around to face Pop again. "And I suppose you think the same thing happened with Becky Mason. Is that it? I was screwing both of them and when they threatened to go to the dean and reveal me, I killed them." He grinned and shook his head, dropping his arms to his sides.

"It's a good theory, I suppose. But you, Mr. Fischer, have a vivid and wild imagination. I wouldn't stoop so low as to have sex with Becky Mason, and Mellie—I could have had sex with her but only if we were about to be married. No, Mr. Fischer, I didn't kill those young ladies. You will have to take my word for that. And furthermore, Mellie would never have threatened to reveal any relationship we might have had to the dean. She was too wonderful to stoop to something like blackmail. Of course, I have no doubts but what Becky Mason would have turned me in had I been so stupid as to get involved with her."

"Hmm," Pop said as he straightened his cap. "I'll keep in touch." He ambled on out of the dual office without even so much as a backward glance. Had he done so he would have seen Professor Jerry Gulf with hands on hips, glaring angrily at him.

18

It was nearly three when Pop Fischer had learned of Carl Watkin's whereabouts at the practice field next to the football stadium. He skirted the hugh edifice in his old Chevrolet and brought the car to rest at the near end of the practice field.

Approximately forty or so players occupied the grassy field and they were dressed in full pads and helmets. Roughly half, Pop estimated, wore red jerseys with silver numerals, silver pants, and silver helmets decorated with a red silhouette of a flying hawk, wings extended in full flight. The remainder of the players wore the same silver helmets and pants but, instead of red jerseys, they were attired in white jerseys with red numerals. Spring practice was evidently in full swing.

Pop ambled along the sidelines and stopped near the fifty-yard line to watch the full-fledged scrimmage. Three coaches were on the field with the players. One was positioned at the end of the scrimmage line and the other two occupied positions in each respective backfield. Another coach stood along the sidelines very near Pop's position.

Pop watched as the red team broke their huddle and

lined up in an offensive formation. The red quarterback, under the center, barked signals. The ball was snapped and the red quarterback pivoted and tucked the ball into the belly of number forty-five. The halfback, number forty-five, exploded into the defensive backfield through a hole which seemed to magically open in the line. The runner gave an oncoming defensive back a juke step and raced on by him only to be hit by another back. He twisted, breaking the tackle, and zipped by the would-be tackler and flashed past the other defendrs. The remaining two defensive backs gave chase but it was no contest. The halfback dashed into the end zone and spiked the ball back over his shoulder as he crossed the end line.

Pop felt a sudden exhiliration. A strong urge to cheer loudly for the runner surged through him but he held his composure. That back must be Carl Watkins, he thought. He sure fits the description.

The red team huddled again, then broke out into another offensive formation. The red quarterback took the snap from center. The two lines clashed. The quarterback ran away from the line of scrimmage and extended the ball to the charging fullback. Then at the last moment he pulled it back and faded deeper to pass. He lofted the ball in a neat, perfect spiral. Number forty-five was racing down the sideline with two defensive backs trying their best to keep up. The ball seemed to float over the heads of the defenders to nestle gently into the out-stretched hands of number forty-five. He ran untouched into the end zone and spiked the ball in a fashion similar to the time before.

Pop walked over to the coach that stood near him on the sidelines. Another play had started out on the field and Pop waited for its completion before he spoke. He watched the quarterback hand off to the fullback up through the middle of the line, but this time the defense was equal to the task and swarmed all over the ball carrier before he could gain even a single yard.

As the play ended, Pop stepped forward, flashed his badge, and said, "Name's Fischer, City Constable's Office."

The coach turned his head and stared at Pop. "Wha. . .what did you say? Who are you?"

"Name's Fischer," Pop said. "I'm Chief Constable here in the Cape."

"Oh," the coach said. "I didn't realize, and my mind is on the scrimmage anyway. What can I do for you?" Suddenly, his face took on a knowing look, and his gray eyes beneath bushy eyebrows opened wide. "You're here about that girl that was killed a couple of days ago aren't you?"

"Hmm," Pop said. "You got a player name of Carl Watkins?"

The coach looked as if he didn't understand, then nodded. "Surely, you don't think that Watkins is involved do you? Why, he's our whole offense. With Watkins carrying the ball, we got the best chance we ever had of having an undefeated season next fall. Watkins is a nice guy. He likes girls, sure. Most young guys do. But he'd never kill one. Not Watkins!"

Pop shrugged his shoulders. "Didn't say he is involved. He's got information about a killin' though, and I'd like to talk to him for a spell if you can spare him long enough."

"Well, sure. Just as long as he's not involved. We sure can't afford to lose him. Not with his potential. Man, he's a beaut.'

"Didn't say he wasn't involved at all," Pop said. "He's a suspect just like several other students on this campus. But I ain't made up my mind as to who done it

157

as yet. When that time comes, you'll know about it, if it's Watkins."

The coach turned toward the field. "Hey, Watkins, come here will yuh?" He looked at Pop. "For sure, he ain't in any trouble now is he? We really need him bad next year."

"Can't rightly say, but mebbe. Yuh never can tell."

A stocky Negro, wearing number forty-five, broke away from the huddle and trotted over to the sidelines. "You want me, coach?" He pulled off his helmet and tucked it under his arm.

"The Constable here wants to talk to you," the coach said.

"Constable? Constable! You must of come because of Becky Mason. Geeze. I ain't involved in that."

Pop motioned with his head toward the stands. "Can we talk over there?"

"Yeah. I guess so."

Pop glanced sideways at him as they walked toward the stands.

"You seem to be a purty good running back from the looks of what I've seen here."

The boy smiled broadly, exposing pearly-white teeth. "I do all right. I guess it's just a special knack for me. Comes easy. I just get that ole ball and run, twist and turn and nobody can hang on to me. I like it. It's fun."

"Heard you might make All-American."

"Yeah. I'm counting on that. I should be a cinch for Class three. This is a small school, but I think I've even got a hell of a chance to win the Heisman next year."

"You're that good are you?" Pop said.

"Yeah. I think so and so do the coaches."

They reached the stands and Pop sat down on the steps leading to the first tier of seats. Watkins looked around as if he might find something more comfortable.

Then he took a seat beside Pop and set his helmet on the ground.

"You didn't come here to talk to me about my football abilities now did you? No, sir. You came over here to ask me what I know about the death of Becky Mason. Now ain't that right?"

"Tis," Pop said. He dug out his pipe and filled it. He scratched a kitchen match along the concrete step and applied the flame to the loaded pipe. After it was burning well, he turned to Watkins and asked, "You dated the Mason girl some, didn't you?"

"Yeah, man. We had a sort of steady thing goin' there for a while. We'd go out three, four times a week. But the last couple of weeks it had cooled off some. I didn't even see her on the day she got killed." He ran his large hands over the legs of his football pants, but he wouldn't look at Pop.

"Mind if I ask a personal question?" Pop asked.

Watkins looked at him in surprise not sure whether the old man was putting him or not. "No. I guess not," he said simply.

"You get intimate with her, did yuh?"

"Intimate? You mean did I screw her. Yeah, I tumbled her a few times. She was like a nymph, man. I mean she wanted it all the time. I couldn't make her happy for very long, because she was right back at me. You know what I mean?"

"She drop you?" Pop asked.

"Did she drop me! Hell, no! No honky chick is gonna drop Carl Watkins. Man, I just got tired of her. I told her I was gonna find me some strange stuff, but if she was good to ole Carl, that I'd come by every once in a while and make her feel good. I mean, man, the girls chase Carl, not the other way around."

"Hmm," Pop said. "You know a kid name of

159

Frankie Rathlich?''

''Frankie? Yeah, I know the skinny little runt. Why, man?''

''You know he was datin' Becky Mason?''

''Sure, man. I knew he was goin' around with Becky. So what? If she liked the skinny sonofabitch that was her business.''

''That your real reaction?''

''Real reaction? What the hell do you mean?'' He pulled at an earlobe. ''What that slut did on her own time didn't matter a damn to me, man. Just as long as she provided when she was with me. That's all that really counted.''

''Hmm,'' Pop muttered. He tapped the ashes from his pipe on the concrete step and returned it to his sweater pocket.

''Did you ever have any intentions of marrying her?''

Watkins roared with laughter. ''Now, where did you get that notion? Man, you is somethin' else. When ole Carl gets married, he's gonna settle down with a sister not no white trash. And that's for damn sure!''

Pop nodded and reached for his pipe again. ''That strange stuff, as you put it, that wouldn't be Melba Stuart now would it?''

''Melba Stuart? Man, you jivin' me ain'tcha? Melba's a real hoity-toity broad, man. You know what I mean? Hell, she's a bigot. She just doesn't go for us niggers. Shit!''

''Not like Becky Mason then?''

''No way, man. No way.'' He folded his arms. ''When it comes to stiff cock, man, Becky was color blind. Not that Stuart board. Her tushy was too precious. She was savin' it, man.''

''Watkins, did you know that a girl was killed in the science building last night?'' Pop applied another match to his pipe.

Watkins worried the sod with a cleted shoe. "Another girl, huh? Nope, I don't know anything about it. Was it somebody I knew?"

"Hmm," Pop said, applying another fire to his pipe. "Witness says he saw you come out of the building about the right time."

"What time was that, man?"

"About ten-thirty or there abouts."

"Ten-thirty? Let me see, ten-thirty? Yeah, sure. I was there all right, but I didn't kill no girl, man." He leaned back and looked at Pop with a surprised expression on his face which slowly melted into a frown. "So that's it, huh. Rollins finked didn't he? I seen him on the bridge with some chick last night, man. And I didn't see nobody else that I can remember. That bastard finked!"

"What time did you see him?"

"Like you said, man, about ten-thirty. I'd just finish-ed a chemistry experiment and was on my way back to the dorm when I met them."

"Could the girl have been Melba Stuart?"

"Yeah. I guess it could have been Melba all right. In fact, I'm positive it was Melba now that you mention it."

"You have a key to the building?"

"Sure, man, I got a key. All us chemistry majors got keys. We got to take care of our experiments at odd hours. Why?"

"No reason. What time did you get back to the dorm?"

"Just shortly after I saw Rollins and Melba. It's only a five minute walk from the science building."

"Anyone corroborate the time you returned?"

The big black shook his head. "No, man. My room-mate got in about twelve. He can tell you I was there

161

then.''

"Hmm," Pop said as he stoked his pipe.

"Who was the girl that got wasted, anyhow?" Watkins asked.

"Melba Stuart," Pop said, digging his hands into his sweater pockets and sucking on his pipe.

"Hey, man, you don't mean it? Melba was all right—a good chick. She was a little hung up over color but other than that she was okay." Suddenly, Watkins stood up. "Hey, man. You tryin' to lay this on me? Rollins was walking with that chick toward the science building. You'd better ask that white sonofabitch was he the one that done it and leave off hasslin' me."

A football bounced nearby. Watkins walked over and picked it up and fired it back toward the middle of the field. A whistle shrilled and the sound of plastic impacting against plastic cracked across the field.

"That Rollins cat plays with all the chicks, and his old lady sits home every night thinking he's bustin' his brain in the library. You go talk to him, old man, and don't mess with me no more. I ain't taking the rap for that honky Don Juan and that's for damn sure." He turned and trotted back out onto the field.

Pop tapped out his pipe and shoved it back into his pocket. Then he slowly pushed himself erect. Carl wore his feelings on his sleeve. It was obvious that he had some strong emotions about his relationship with Becky Mason, but Pop wasn't sure just how he related to Melba Stuart. He seemed to be a little upset that she had never gone out with him. Of course, he'd covered his feelings pretty good after Pop told him she'd been the one who was killed in the science building last night. Well, he still wasn't any closer to an answer but one was coming, he could feel it. It was only a matter of time now and the killer would be his. He shambled off toward his ancient Chevrolet.

19

The sun was a bright red disk sinking into the western horizon when Pop Fischer finally arrived back at police headquarters. He wasn't sure whether or not the day had been fruitful. He'd spent a dern sight of time talking to folks and that was for sure. He could already feel the pressure. Claude Dale was rantin' and ravin' at Mayor Olson and there wasn't a thing he could do. Well, if he had his way he's just let Dale have his tantrum and ignore him, but Mayor Olson couldn't really afford to do that—not on his behalf. He'd have to act and soon. If only he could remember that one little item he'd passed over too quickly. But try as best he could, he just couldn't seem to dredge it up. He'd just have to keep racking his brain and see what he could find and keep on askin' questions. He wasn't going to let Mayor Olson down.

He twisted the knob and walked into headquarters. Carmody was already at his station behind the desk. Thank heaven for that much. At least he wouldn't have to deal with that pesky female and her continuous run of questions.

Carmody looked up at him and frowned. He said

nothing but returned to the paperback book he was reading, ignoring Pop.

"Evenin'," Pop said as he walked on by the desk and into the office. Carmody acknowledged him with a nod.

Macklin wasn't here which surprised him. Now where do you suppose that young whelp is, he thought. Maybe since he'd put Macklin on days, he'd gone home already. No, that wasn't it, he was sure. He wouldn't quit while he was still out. No, he'd wait just to see what he would have to say. He stepped back into the main room.

"Where's Macklin?"

Carmody looked up and adjusted his foot on the flyleaf of the desk. "Where do you expect? He's over at the diner makin' goo goo eyes at Connie." Carmody didn't wait for an answer or even an acknowledgement but went back to his book as if he were right in the middle of the most exciting part and couldn't bear to leave it even long enough to carry on a conversation with Pop.

Pop entered the diner which was located directly across the street from the court house. It was filled to capacity with the usual late evening crowd. He looked about for Connie, one of the night waitresses, and the one Macklin usually came to talk to. But Connie wasn't anywhere to be seen. It was probably too early for her. He continued to search the interior of the restaurant until he finally spotted Macklin at a booth by himself with his back towrd the door. Pop shambled over and took the seat opposite Macklin.

"Did you catch the evening news?" Macklin asked.

"Nope," Pop said.

"They had Claude Dale on. He was sure givin' you and Mayor Olson hell. He said you were too old and senile and incompetent to conduct a murder investigation. And how the Mayor wouldn't retire you. He said

164

we'd never get to the bottom of these homicides and every coed on campus is in danger."

"So, he's started has he. Well, we'll just have to fix him good. Olson ain't gonna do anything and, in short time, we're gonna make a fool of Mr. Claude Dale. Yes, sir. He's shootin' his mouth off and I aim to make him sorry."

Macklin grinned. "How'd the day go?" Macklin asked. "Find anything worthwhile?"

"Not much. Got three prime suspects talked to today. None of 'em had a solid alibi."

Maybelle, a plump, jolly waitress, appeared at the side of the booth. "What can I get for the Cape's finest?" she asked.

Macklin winked at her, and her pudgy cheeks turned a rosy-red.

"Make mine a steak," Pop said without looking up.

"I'll have the same," Macklin said.

"I suppose you want coffee, Len?" She looked at Macklin. He nodded. "And you, no doubt, want a cup of hot water?"

Pop grinned and said, "Yup. Can't eat a meal without my hot water."

Maybelle waddled away toward the kitchen and Pop turned to Macklin. He related his interrogations of the day.

Macklin sat, looking perplexed.

"Rollins was lyin'," he said. "I checked out that flat tire he was supposed to have had, but the night man at the Texaco said nobody brought in a flat last night."

Macklin was still looking thoughtful. Finally, he said, "For my money it's that geology professor."

"Mebbe so—mebbe so. It's too early to be sure."

Maybelle set two steaming steaks before them, and both men immediately dug in.

Chewing steak, Macklin said, "What if I'm right about that geology professor? He might just kill him another one tonight!"

"Possible," Pop said as he bit into a heavily-buttered biscuit. "Got a tail on him?"

"Nope," Macklin said, grinning mischeviously.

It was Pop's turn to looked perplexed. He knows somethin', he thought. There's somethin' he knows that he ain't told me yet. Well, I'll just wait him out. He'll get around to it directly. Pop pushed his plate away and searched for his pipe.

Macklin sipped his coffee, still gloating.

"There's a little something naggin' at the back of my mind. Something I've passed over. When I get it out in the open, we'll have our man," Pop said, lighting his pipe. "What's the story on the Stuart girl?"

"Got it right here," Macklin said, handing a folded sheaf of papers to his superior.

Pop tucked them into his back pocket without looking at them. "I'll read it in the mornin'," he said. "How'd it go? Did Doc Spelchur come up with any new ideas?"

"Nope. Nothing really new. It went pretty much like the other one. Doc said she had semen and Vaseline in her vagina just like the other one. Only this time there was a little blood mixed with the Vaseline and semen. Doc said he figured she was a virgin."

"Could he tell if she'd been raped," Pop asked.

"Doc said he couldn't tell for sure. He said her hymen was torn but otherwise there was no indication of a forceful entry. He said as far as he could tell she hadn't been raped."

"Interestin'," Pop said.

"The cause of death was by strangulation just like the Mason girl. The bruises were different like he said this

166

morning. Otherwise, everything was the same except he left her with a bra and a sweatshirt.''

"Oh, so now it's a he is it?" Pop chortled. "That ain't gonna suit Jill at all unless it's Carl Watkins."

Macklin laughed. "I guess I just assumed it'd be a him. But now that you mention it, that Landsberg girl is strong enough to have done it. You know, I think she should have been a man."

"There's truth in that," Pop said.

Pop sat back and drank the last of his hot water which was now merely tepid. He puffed thoughtfully on his pipe.

Macklin traced rings on the table top with his coffee cup. Then suddenly his face lit up. "Damn! I almost forgot. Riley found a jar of Vaseline in Gulf's desk this afternoon."

"What!" Pop said, dropping his pipe on the table. "Did he have a search warrant?"

"Nope. He was just nosing around, he said. He left it where it was. Said if you wanted he'd get a warrant and go get it. It's too late for that now, I guess."

"It'll keep. Gulf didn't see him did he? I mean he didn't tip Gulf to what he was doing?"

"Nope. Gulf was in class and he'd left his office open. Riley just went there on a hunch."

"What was Riley doin' over there anyhow?" Pop asked.

"Who knows?" Macklin said. "You know how Riley thinks of himself as a master detective. He probably wanted to break the case for you."

"Hmm," Pop said. "We'll go get it come mornin'. You might take that little task on yourself." Pop retrieved his precious cap. "I'm gonna sleep on it. See you in the mornin'.'"

20

Fenton Riley edged the patrol car in next to the curb, being careful to keep it just outside the cone of light shed by the street lamp. Step-like terraces stretched upward toward the top of the knoll where the gray stone structure of the administration building seemed to be balanced. Trees, growing randomly from the loessal soil, enshrouded the back of the administration building and kept the ridge in deep shadow. The night was quiet and no one seemed to be about. Somewhere a cicada thrummed hypnotically and Riley felt alone in his world.

He pulled a pint bottle of Old Bushmills from beneath the front seat. It still contained about three-fourths of its original contents. He unscrewed the cap, tilted the bottle and took a long pull of the amber fluid. He was piqued at Pop Fischer and Leonard Macklin for the duty change which had disrupted his normal daily routine. The unknown killer also drew a part of his animosity. Why didn't Fischer expedite the investigation and arrest that goddamned geology professor so he could get back into his usual lackadaisical routine. Hell, Fischer was probably prolonging the whole investigation just to make him miserable. It had to be the geology professor. The Vaseline proved that. He swallowed another generous swig of the whiskey, wiped his mouth in satisfaction with the back of his hand, and shoved the bottle back under the seat.

The routine of the department was fairly loosely structured and Riley normally worked the eight to four shift. Tim Collier had the four to midnight stint, and Spence Ferguson, the newest man on the force, had the midnight to eight shift. Instead of rotating them from shift to shift, Pop assigned them according to seniority, and since Riley had been on the force for four years, he drew the day patrol. The relief for the three of them came from two part-time officers who worked only three shifts each per week. Both of the part-timers had been employed by security agencies before they had settled in Cape Collins to retire. Mike Kelly, in his mid-sixties, had worked for the Pinkerton Detective Agency in Detroit, and Porter Clinton, also in his mid-sixties, had been employed by Wackenhut in Boston for thirty years or so. The job provided a nice diversion for the retirees as well as providing relief time for the force's regular officers.

Riley felt put upon in this specific case because Pop had altered their routine duty. Riley was now working a twelve-hour shift from noon until midnight when Ferguson took over to work from midnight to noon. Collier had an overlapping shift, extending from four in the afternoon until four in the morning. This way Fischer could insure that the campus was heavily patrolled at all times except during the early morning and daylight hours. The times he felt another murder was very unlikely.

Riley brought the bottle out for another jolt, then

pushed it back to its hiding place. He breathed a sigh of contentment and leaned back to relax. Well, his shift was almost over, he thought, and he could count on meeting Ferguson at the station house at midnight. If there was anything about that nigger, he was prompt, and Riley took solace in that. He sighed again and closed his eyes as he began to feel the effect of the booze.

Riley was a big man. He had a stocky build and stood only five feet nine in his stocking feet. His musculature was ill defined which gave him a soft, flabby appearance. But the soft, pudgy look was misleading for it belied his strength—a strength which was easily equivalent to that of two ordinary men his size.

Riley had spent eight years in the army in the military police where he had an easy-going, not-too-demanding duty. It suited his outlook on life, particularly that part of it devoted to work. He had made sergeant before his discharge at the end of his second tour of duty and, at one point, he had considered making the army a career. However, at the last moment he had turned down the second re-enlistment bonus and had entered civilian life with no definite plans in mind.

His first civilian job had been with a roofing crew but his sensitive skin, which was a product of his red hair and fair complexion that went along with it, burned easily. He had worked through most of the summer even though most of the time he had burned and peeled, burned and peeled again over and over. Then the job on the police force had opened and he applied, confident that his tenure in the MPs would garner him the job. That had been four years ago and now he was settled into a job he really liked. He rode around in a squad car all day which was an easy way to make a living, with no

170

more crime than there was in Cape Collins. The job also gave him a certain amount of respect on the part of the populace which he couldn't have commanded without the job and the uniform.

Well, might as well get to it, he thought. The whiskey under the seat entered his mind, and his mouth watered. A moment of indecision gripped him, then he succumbed and pulled the bottle out once more and took a long drink. He belched with satisfaction, replaced the bottle, opened the door and stepped into the street. He pulled the seat of his pants out of his crotch, picked up his flashlight and locked the car door.

He climbed the terraces and walked through a wooded area to the walk that led to the science building. The sky was overcast with slate-gray clouds, making his surroundings much lighter than they would have been under a clear, moonless sky. There was enough dim, gray light that he really didn't need the flashlight he carried. However, he might find a use for it later on and he hadn't yet turned it on.

The campus was quiet. Nothing or no one stirred. Riley was all alone in a shadowed world. The bridge across the ravine beckoned to him and he started across. He paused mid-way and shined the flashlight down into the entertwined shadows of the ravine. There was nothing there other than the chunks of brick-studded concrete.

Damn that killer, he thought. If it weren't for him, he could be at home right now and cozily drunk. His mouth watered as he thought of the bottle back in the car. He didn't know why they had him patrolling a deserted campus. So two girls had been killed. So what? Did they expect to find a murdered girl every night in this goddamned hole in the ground. He swung the flashlight over on the other side of the bridge, but just like before there was nothing to be seen. He walked on across the bridge and took a turn around the science building. Still, he found nothing. There were no lights on in the building other than the night safety lights which spread an eerie glow. There wasn't anybody out tonight, not with the hint of rain in the air. Pausing, he looked once more at the science building but still there was nothing.

He walked across the bridge. Then out of curiosity he made his way down into the gorge to have a look around. The fill was scattered in such a way that there were many little nooks and crannies where his light would not reach from up on the bridge. He clambered over the chunks of concrete, shining the light from place to place. Satisfied that there was no body hidden in the ravine, he started toward the edge. A dark object caught his eye and he moved toward it. Shining the light on the object, he recognized it as a woman's purse. He picked it up. It was large, made of leather with a long strap so that it could be carried over the shoulder. He opened it. Inside, he found a snubnosed .38 calibre pistol, odds and ends of make-up and Kleenex, a pencil and a pad of traffice tickets. He flipped open the wallet to find a small silver badge, and an identification card with Jill Readon's picture looking back at him.

"Holy Christ!" he muttered. "The sonofabitch has got Jill." He climbed out of the ravine and ran along the walk, through the wooded area, down the terraces, pulling out his keys as he ran. He opened the door and grabbed the microphone.

"Carmody, this is Riley. Do you read me?"

He waited patiently. There was some static and finally he heard Carmody's voice.

"Yeah, Riley. I hear you. What have you got out there? Another dead coed?"

"Hell, no! I found Jill Readon's purse."

"So? Where'd you find it?"

"In the goddamned ravine!"

"Oh, oh. So that bitch has been investigating on her own has she. Well, what do you know. Serves her right poking her nose in where she had no business. Them murder cases is the old man's worries not her's. Shit. She got what was comin' to her."

"Carmody, will you call Pop, please?"

"Hell, no. I ain't about to call that old bastard. I'll call Macklin for ya and if he wants to call Pop that's his goose."

Riley hung the microphone back in the holder and reached for the purse. He extracted the wallet and looked it over again as if he were trying to be certain it was Jill's. There was no doubt about who it belonged to. He opened up the compartment where the bills were kept. He counted the money. There were two twenties, a ten, a five and two singles. He took out a twenty and the ten and folded the wallet. Then he thought better of it and removed the other twenty. Together with the other bills he shoved it into his pocket. Hell, he thought, nobody will ever know, and she's probably dead and won't miss the money nohow.

He leaned back in the seat to relax, thought of the bottle and pulled it out from under the seat. Uncapping it, he drank until his eyes teared. He wiped the back of his hand across his mouth, tilted the bottle once more and emptied it. Just then a pair of headlights flashed across his back window. He shoved the empty bottle under the seat and stepped out into the street.

Macklin was coming toward him from his white

Pontiac.

"Carmody said you found Jill's purse," Macklin said.

"Yeah," he said, and reached into the car and brought out the purse and handed it to Macklin.

Macklin examined it carefully. Withdrew the wallet and eyeballed the shield and I.D. card. "It's her's all right."

Riley nodded but said nothing.

Two cars approached from opposite directions. One was a patrol car and the other was a black Ford. Ferguson got out of the black Ford, walked past Macklin's Pontiac to join them. Collier came from the other direction.

"You didn't find any sign of her did you?" Macklin asked.

"No. I sure didn't," Riley said.

"Where'd you look?"

"In the ravine and around the science building. She wasn't anywhere to be seen. I think the bastard has got her somewhere."

"Maybe," Macklin said. "But we've got to be sure. Collier, you go along the other side of that building," Macklin said, pointing to the administration building "and Ferguson, you go up the other side. Riley, you come with me. We'll have a look down the middle of the campus. Spread out some. Look behind every tree, every bush, any place where a body could be hidden. We'll meet at the science building."

Riley followed Macklin, finding it difficult to keep pace with the long-legged deputy. They searched the terraces, scoured the wooded area and the ravine. Riley took the end in the direction of the new girl's gym where the ravine had been filled and landscaped except for about fifty yards from the bridge. Macklin went the other way, down to where the ravine disappeared into another wooded area. They met on the other side.

"Nothin'," Riley said. "Not a damn thing."

"Same here," Macklin said.

"Come on. Let's check the science building," Macklin said, striding off at a rapid pace.

Riley turned left so as to meet Macklin on the other side. Nothing had changed. There was nobody stirring, and even though he searched the shrubbery diligently he found no sign that anyone had been anywhere near the place with a dead or incapacitated woman.

On the other side, he met Macklin and the latter tried the door.

"Locked," Macklin muttered.

"Both doors are locked," Riley said. "I tried 'em both before and they were both locked."

"Maybe, I'd better call Pop," Macklin said uncertainly. "He can get us a key. I think we need to look inside."

Riley coughed into his hands. Damn, he sure didn't want Pop to come out here. The old man, he was pretty sure, suspected he drank on duty. Now all he had to do was catch him at it. Shit! He had the damnedest luck.

A car careened around the corner and came racing across the parking lot, throwing limestone chips, and shuddered to a halt not twenty yards away from them.

A tall, dark-haired man with plastic-rimmed glasses resting on his nose leaped from the car and shouted. "Who are. . ." He paused and calmned a bit. "Oh, the police."

It was Macklin's turn to inquire. "Just who are you?"

"Well! I'm Bryan Turner, dean of this university,

that's who. Mrs. Grayson, who lives over there," he said, pointing in the direction from which he had come, "called me and said there were some men lurking about the science building. So, naturally, I came along to find out what is going on."

"Naturally," Macklin said. "A policewoman's purse was found in the ravine awhile ago. We think some foul play has befallen her. No doubt, it was our killer striking again." Macklin turned toward the building. "Do you have a key to this building?"

"Why, of course. I have master keys for every building on this campus. Do you want to look inside?"

Collier and Ferguson joined them, and the dean looked at them with a disapproving look.

"Yes, it's imperative that we search the building," Macklin said.

"Very well," Turner said. He returned to his cars and came back with a ring filled with keys. He fumbled through them, selected one, tried it, tried a second and finally pulled the door open.

Inside, Macklin said, "Collier, you and Ferguson take the second floor, and Riley and I will search this floor. Look in every corner. Look any place a body might be hidden." He turned to Turner and said, "By the way do you have a key for the inside doors?"

Turner nodded and pulled a key from the ring and handed it to Macklin. "I have two master keys that will open the doors in this building as a matter of fact. Shall I accompany these gentlemen?" He gestured at Collier and Ferguson.

Macklin nodded.

They searched every room, every classroom, every office, every laboratory, every restroom, and every storage room. After the search they reassembled at the door.

"Find anything?" Macklin asked.

They shook their heads in unison.

"Well, I guess we'll have to call Pop," Macklin said.

"Wait," Riley said. "Something just occurred to me."

"What's that?" Macklin asked.

"Jill wouldn't walk all the way up here. So where is her car?"

"You've got a point," Macklin said. "It's not on campus, so search the streets and parking areas adjacent to the campus. If you don't find it we can assume that our murderer has it along with Jill. I'll go contact Pop."

Riley left them. He was playing a hunch. He swung the patrol car out into the street and gunned it. Taking the corners on squealing tires, he soon arrived at a shopping center bordering on the west side of the campus. He looked carefully over the parking lot. Just as he'd guessed. There was her little Mustang, parked next to a light pole. He got out and looked it over. Everything seemed to be in order. He fingered the bills in his pocket. Serves the damn bitch right, he thought, a broad grin spreading across his face.

Back in the patrol car, he handled the mike again.

"Carmody, patch me through to Macklin will ya?"

21

The gray morning sky was tinged with pink when Pop Fischer awoke. He lay there contemplating the weird shadows cast upon the ceiling by the early morning light.

Macklin's late night call had roused him from a deep sleep, but he had refused to let Macklin's contagious excitement plague him. If they hadn't found Jill's body, then chances were good that she was still alive. A few more hours—until daylight at least—wouldn't make much difference. So Pop had nonchalantly accepted what Macklin had had to say, then he had told him to get some rest and they would get on it first thing in the morning. Macklin had been adamant about starting a city-wide search that very minute, and for the first time in their relationship, Macklin had argued strongly with him. But Pop had not been moved so easily. There wasn't any use rousting people out of bed in the middle of the night, especially since they still didn't have a clue as to whom it might have been that kidnapped Jill. He had to suppose that it was the same individual that had killed the two girls and that Jill had stumbled on to something that had led the killer to kidnapping her. Why he hadn't killed her was a mystery to Pop. It would all come out in time.

Pop swung his creaking limbs out of bed and stood shakily erect for a moment. Pain was centered in the small of his back and radiated down each leg all the way to the soles of his feet. After a while the numbness began to subside. The pain remained but at least he could now move his legs without stumbling all over the place.

He showered, shaved, and dressed. He pulled on the usual brown wool pants, which bagged around his legs, and a gray sweater with gaping pockets. The sweater was a part of his every day attire except during the highest heat of summer. There were those that assumed that he wore the same sweater every day, but nothing could be further from the truth. Pop had five sweaters, all identical. In fact, he had come upon the sweaters at a sale in a local haberdashery. They had five gray sweaters in his size along with several other colors. But Pop had liked gray so he had bought the five gray sweaters, and the possibility of mixing colors had never occurred to him. So now everyday he wore a gray sweater, changing them weekly to be washed.

He shambled out to the kitchen and put on bacon and eggs to fry. He poured a cup of steaming water from the teakettle on the old range and sat down to eat.

A half hour later Pop walked into Police headquarters. The place looked deserted. Carmody had already gone and there seemed to be no one else about. He found Macklin at his desk, head down on his arms, fast asleep. He chuckled to himself, sat down at his own desk and stoked his first pipe of the morning. When he had it burning well, he turned to Macklin.

"Well, Len," he said. "Any developments since I talked to you last night?"

Macklin sat up abruptly, rubbing sleep from his eyes.

179

His shaggy hair was tousled and his eyes were red-rimmed from lack of sleep.

He stared at Pop. "What? My God! It's about time. We've got to get going and do something quick. That crazy bastard has got Jill somewhere. We don't know how long he's gonna keep her alive. Hell, she may be dead already. He's already killed two girls that we know of so there's nothing to keep him from killing Jill."

"Simmer down, boy. We can't go off in all directions at once. We got to give some thought as to where she might be and just who it is that snatched her." He puffed his pipe for a few minutes, watching Macklin wringing his hands in frustration.

"What we got so far?" Pop asked.

"What do you mean, what have we got so far?"

"Easy, boy. You're gonna bust a blood vessel if you don't simmer down some. Now, let's think about what we know for sure up to now. Then maybe we'll know which direction to go."

"Oh, shit! I don't feel like playing games this morning. We've got to find Jill. Can't you understand that, her life is in danger!"

"We ain't aplayin' games, boy. I'm dead serious and don't you forget it. I'm as deeply concerned about that gal's well-being as you are but I'm gonna find which way we should turn afore I go off makin' arrests. And, if I'm gonna do that, I got to hash over the facts we got so far. I'm tryin' my damndest to figger out which ever way we should go—where we need to look. Now, will you cooperate with me?"

"I suppose," Macklin said, jamming his fist into his palm. "Hey, I got a better idea. Let's bring in our five suspects. That way we'll have them here in front of us and as long as we do Jill will be safe." He leaned back again, a satisfied grin on his face.

Pop pulled the pipe from his mouth and swung around and placed his elbows on the desk. Macklin had a point. He might even be about ready to take over for him, but he'd have to wait and see. Macklin had to mature into the chief's job some day, and Pop was growing tired of waiting. But right now threre were more pressing problems that needed his attention.

Pop reached over and picked up the phone and dialed a number. To Macklin, he said, "Call Clinton and tell him to go pick up Gulf and bring him down here. Get Ferguson on the radio and have him go get Rollins." Into the phone he said, "Hello, Mike?" He listened for a moment, then said, "Go over to the dorm on campus and pick up that Rathlich kid and bring him down here."

Macklin hung up the phone.

"Len, you go get that Landsberg gal, and I'll call Riley to go pick up Watkins. We'll get 'em all down here together and see if we can pick out a killer."

Macklin left at a rapid pace approximating a run as if each and every moment was precious.

Time dragged by as he waited for his deputies to bring in the five suspects. He didn't know what good it would do to have them here in front of him except that Jill might be protected in that way. Well who knows, he thought, if he had them here where he could talk to them, something good might come out of it. Something one of them might say could possibly lead him to the one that had Jill stashed away. He felt reasonably sure that Jill was still alive and that her body wasn't going to turn up. No, one of them had her held prisoner somewhere—somewhere in town, and he was going to find out who and damned soon.

While he waited he called upstairs and ordered a search warrant for Gulf's residence. While he was questioning them would be a good time for his deputies to be searching his place. They might just be lucky enough to turn up Jill. Certainly, if it were Rollins, Rathlich, Watkins or Landsberg they wouldn't turn up anything. They couldn't have a captive secluded in their dorm rooms or in married-student housing.

The first to arrive was Porter Clinton with an irate Jerry Gulf in tow. Gulf's face was cherry-red with anger and his fists were clenched at his sides.

"Goddamnit, old man! What the hell is going on? You pull me out of the classroom in the middle of the morning. Couldn't whatever is troubling you wait until I was through?" Gulf was sputtering. He continued his tirade at Pop at an almost shout, filled with tense anger. "Am I under arrest?" he gurgled. "Because if I am, you'd better make it good, old man. Because I'm going to bring a law suit against you and that's for damn sure. You can't go around harassing innocent citizens."

"Calm down, boy. No, you ain't under arrest—not jest yet, leastwise. I just had you brought down here so I can ask you a few questions that need answerin' bad."

"Couldn't it wait until another time? Damn! Right in the middle of class a cop pulls me out of the room like a common criminal. What in hell do you think the students are thinking? Jesus Christ, man! I have work to do."

"Nope. These questions couldn't wait," Pop said. "We got us a little bit of a rush on this mornin'. Now, you find you a comfortable chair out there in the main room and I'll be out there directly." He dismissed Gulf with a nod of his head and began shuffling papers on his desk.

Gulf threw up his hands in exasperation, walked out of the office and took a chair under the windows that faced on Harrison Street.

Moments later Kelly came in, marching Frankie Rathlich before him. The kid was pale and shaking with fear. He did his best not to look Gulf in the eye and he took his seat without question, three chairs away from Jerry Gulf. Gulf, likewise, ignored him.

Ferguson had been near the campus when the call had come to him over the radio. He had had a little trouble with Rollins at first, but Ferguson wasn't one to fool with belligerent suspects. He had his orders and that was to bring Rollins in. As soon as he had shown that his strength was superior to Rollins's, he'd had no more trouble and he came along docily. At headquarters, Rollins took a seat next to Gulf.

"Dr. Gulf! My God. They've got you too. What do they think they are doing? Why are we here?"

"Who knows? Ask the old man in there. He has it in his mind that one of us killed Becky and Mell. . . Melba." Gulf folded his arms across his chest, stretched his feet out and crossed them at the ankles. Then he lapsed into silence. Rollins looked sideways at Rathlich who was staring at his knees. Rollins shrugged and slouched in his chair to await whatever was coming.

Mackling was next to come in. Betty Landsberg was walking stiff and straight about one step ahead of Macklin. A cigaret was dangling from her lower lip. As they came in the door, she slowed, looking in wonder at the ones who were assembled there ahead of her. Macklin clasped her arm gently just above the elbow in an attempt to steer her alone toward a chair.

"Get your fuckin' hands off me, pig! I came along with you, but you don't put your hands on me. Is that clear?" She sat down two chairs on the far side of Rathlich and inhaled deeply on her cigaret and blew smoke ceilingward. She paid no mind to the others who were obviously in here for the same reason she was.

183

They waited impatiently, suspects and policemen alike. Pop Fischer remained in his office. During the whole time, no one spoke, but if looks could kill, the Cape would need a new police force. Finally, Riley came in pushing a reluctant Carl Watkins before him. Once inside Watkins dug his hands deep into his pockets, glowered at the line of deputies, and swaggered over to take a seat next to Frankie Rathlich. As he surveyed the others a mischievous grin broke out over his face.

Rathlich inched away from the black as if he thought Watkins had taken the chair next to him so that he might do him some bodily harm if the opportunity arose.

Pop entered the lobby from his office with a document in his hand. He handed the paper to Mike Kelly and said, "Mike, you and Porter execute this will ya?"

Kelly saluted the old man, took the paper, glanced at Clinton, and left.

"I see everybody's here," Pop said, looking around the room.

"Get on with it," Gulf said, irritated. "Whatever it is you're doing this morning."

"I intend to," Pop said, lighting the ever-present pipe. "Now let's see. None of you have alibis and all of you were associated with both Rebecca Mason and Melba Stuart. I suspect, too, that if we dig enough we can find a motive for each of you. That's what we're gonna do this mornin' bring it all out in the open." He paused and half sat on Jill's desk. Would it be best to mention Jill's disappearance or would it be better to just forge ahead and let things fall as they would. Well, he'd have to decide and quick.

He looked each in the eyes for a few seconds. All

except Frankie Rathlich who was still studying his knees.

Finally, folding his arms, he frowned and said, "We've got our policewoman missin'. Her purse was found in the ravine last night. Any of you know anything about that?" He really didn't expect an answer, and all he got in return was hard stares from those that would look at him.

It was no use. This wasn't his way. He wasn't even sure that he should have them all grouped together like this. Things that they said might be interpreted as invasion of privacy, but in the predicament they faced, it looked as if it was going to be necessary to interrogate them together. But he wasn't the one to do it. Besides, if he sat off and didn't take part, he might catch something which he might otherwise miss. Of course, he couldn't lead them along, but he could butt in if necessary. And it was time he started giving a little more responsibility to Macklin. Yes, that was it. Let Macklin do it. It might indicate to him whether Macklin was ready to take over the chief's job yet. He almost wished that Claude Dale was here to witness this. No, that wasn't fair. He was already predicting that Macklin would fail. Well, if it was because he knew or thought that he knew that this interrogation would lead nowhere, he was justified. It might lead to something, but he was doubting it by the minute.

He motioned Macklin over for a short conference in the office. Once inside he drew Macklin close and whispered, "Len, you got to lead the interrogation. It just ain't my style, working with a whole group of folks. Besides you need to take on a little more responsibility here, since it looks as if I ain't gonna be chief much longer—not unless somethin' breaks."

185

'But—'' Macklin said.

"No buts,'' Pop said. "You're gonna do it. Now come on.''

Pop led the way out of the office, pushed through the gate of the rail divider, and sat down at Jill's desk.

Macklin paced the floor in front of the suspects who all eyed him coldly—all except Frankie Rathlich.

Pop wasn't sure if Macklin were nervous or if he was just planning a means of approach, At last he stopped pacing and looked over the group.

"Gulf,'' he said.

Gulf sat up straight and gave Macklin an icy stare but he said nothing.

"Gulf, if you were sexually involved with those two students that could be enough motive to kill. If they threatened to expose you to the dean or any other administrator, it might be just enough motive to murder them. Being sexually involved with students could ruin your career—not only lose you your job, but end your career as a geologist.''

Gulf smiled. "Don't you think that murder would do a great deal more to end my career than simple carnal knowledge of two students?''

"Not if you thought you could get away with it. Besides, you are a prime suspect because of the Vaseline.''

"Vaseline! What Vaseline? What are you talking about?'' The lacy edge of anger was showing again.

"The jar of Vaseline we found in your desk drawer. Don't play coy. It implicates you.''

"I didn't have a jar of Vaseline in my desk. Besides, what does Vaseline have to do with Becky and Melba?''

"Oh, yes, there was a jar of Vaseline in your desk, and a good portion of it had been used.''

"If there was a jar of Vaseline in my desk, it was a plant. I have no need for that sort of thing. Anyway, I fail to see how it ties in with the two girls."

"Ah, ha!" Macklin said. "Both girls had sexual intercourse shortly before they were killed, and Vaseline was found in their vaginas. Does that tie it in for you?"

"Oh! I see. But as I said before, I don't use Vaseline for anything and I assure you that I did not at any time take sexual liberties with either of those two girls."

Macklin was perplexed. He cupped his chin in his hand and rested his elbow on is other arm and began to pace once more.

Again he stopped. "Watkins!" The black glared at him. "Watkins, we know that you dated the Mason girl—quite frequently as a matter of fact. We also know that you tried to date the Stuart girl, but she turned you down."

Frankie Rathlich sat up abruptly and glared at Watkins. His hands, lying along his thighs, were knotted into small fists.

Macklin continued. "We also know that the Mason girl was dating Frankie here. Now, that might have made you angry enough to kill her. The fact that the Stuart girl wouldn't date you, and that you saw her with Rollins that night might have riled you enough to commit murder number two. In fact, I think you are a white-hater. That, perhaps, is the only reason you dated white girls—to rile the whites. And to be rejected by something you hate would be enough for you to kill to my way of thinking."

"You honky bastard!" Watkins screeched. He charged Macklin. Ferguson moved swiftly and threw a shoulder into the black's midsection. The impact hurtled Ferguson back against the rail-divider, flipped him over backward to land on all fours on the other side. Macklin deftly sidestepped the charging halfback like a matador eluding a furious bull. As the black rushed past, Macklin chopped the edge of his hand down against the boy's neck. Watkins crashed to the floor and lay still.

Moments later the dazed Watkins picked himself up and eased his lean, hard body into a chair. He looked dazed, but the violence was completely drained out of him.

Macklin looked at Pop, but he merely shook his head. So Macklin proceeded.

"Rathlich."

The obviously frightened boy gripped the arms of the wooden chair with both hands, causing his knuckles to turn white.

"Honest, Mr. Macklin, I didn't do it," he stammered.

"You had reason though, didn't you? You were in love with Becky Mason now, weren't you?"

"Yes," he said sheepishly. His face was growing paler by the second.

"Just to know that Becky was dating a black could have been motive enough for you to kill her. Isn't that so, Frankie?"

"No, no," he sobbed. "I loved Becky. I couldn't ever hurt her."

"You also had strong feelings for Melba Stuart. I imagine that if you saw her having relations with someone else that might lead you to kill her too. Particularly, if you had already killed once. The second time would have been much easier, now wouldn't it?"

"No, no!" He was now sobbing brokenly and he held his face in his hands to hide the tears.

"Well, Rollins. I mustn't forget you, the campus playboy."

Rollins said nothing, only examined his fingernails.

"It would seem that you are intimate with a large number of coeds on this campus. Particularly, you seem to have a penchant for geology students, and both Rebecca Mason and Melba Stuart were in laboratory sections that you taught. Did you offer them grades in return for sexual favors? You were in a good position to do so."

"No," Rollins said calmly. "I flirted with both those girls. That's just my way. But I assure you that I have never been unfaithful to my wife."

"Why should we believe you? You've lied to us before, Rollins. How am I supposed to know you're not lying now? You lied to us about a flat tire, when, in fact, you had no flat tire. What were you doing that night? Did you spend it with Melba Stuart? We know you were with her; that you walked across campus with her to the science buiding. In fact, you may have been the last one to see her alive. Did you kill her?"

"No, I didn't kill her nor Becky for that matter." He was calm—not in the least perturbed by the situation. "As to what I was doing that night, that is my own personal business and I don't see a need to reveal my whereabouts just yet."

"You may need to. Because you have no alibi and the fact that you were with her makes you a prime candidate for homicide."

"When it comes time, I'll reveal my whereabouts, and you can be certain I will have an air-tight alibi. But until you charge me with murder, I see no reason to reveal where I went and what I did after I left Melba at the science building."

189

"Easily said," Macklin rasped. "But I think maybe you are lying to us again."

Rollins shrugged his shoulders.

Macklin glanced at Pop again, but the old man was as stone-faced as ever.

"As for you, Miss Landsberg."

"Ms., please. If you address me, address me as Ms. Landsberg."

"All right, Ms. Landsberg. You have been a roommate to both of these girls. We know you had a lesbian affair with one of them. Granted we don't know what your relationship was with the other, but we can assume that jealousy here was sufficient motive."

"So what, stud. You've proved nothing," she said.

"That's right!" Gulf said. "All you've done here today is make accusations that you cannot back up. And for what reason? More than likely just to harass us. Well, if you want to charge one of us do it or let us go. It seems all you have done is to indicate that any one of us could have killed those girls. So which of us did it? Make a charge or let us go."

"He's right," Pop said, standing up slowly. "Take 'em home boys," he said to Riley and Ferguson. "We ain't got enough to charge anyone of them with."

After the deputies had left with the suspects, Macklin faced Pop. "Well?" he said.

Pop shook his head. "I don't think we accomplished a thing except to open ourselves to a lot of problems if they should want to press charges. I don't think we should have done it that way, but I figgered somethin' might come of it."

"Hell!" Macklin slammed his fist into his open palm. "We aren't any closer to finding Jill than we were before."

Just then Kelly and Clinton came in. "We didn't find a thing. Everything seems to be in order," Kelly said.

Pop nodded, then turned and went into his office and sat down. Macklin followed and took a seat at his own desk. Pop pulled another pipe from the rack, packed it and lit it. He sat there smoking silently.

Presently, he looked over at Macklin who had his elbows resting on the desk with his head in his hands. A very dejected looking individual, Pop thought.

"How long they been gone?" Pop asked.

"I don't know. About forty-five minutes, I guess. Why?"

"Just wondering how long we'd been settin' here. Damn! The key to this whole puzzle is locked up in my head somewhere. If only I could get it out!" He felt very frustrated.

Suddenly, he snapped his fingers. "Key! Well, I'll be dadburned. So that's it. The key! Tell him to get here quick." He grabbed the telephone book and began leafing through it.

"Quick, boy. We ain't got a minute to lose. We may be too late already!"

22

Macklin caught Pop's change in mood almost immediately. Whatever had been troubling the old man these last few days—whatever it was that he had been digging for must have come to the surface. He had definitely made some sort of decision and, whatever it was, he would get around to telling him about it in due time.

Macklin had tried to fathom this secretiveness the old man had about him on a number of occasions but he had never been able to come up with a conclusive answer. Ultimately, he had attributed it to Pop's penchant for accuracy. If he didn't tell anyone what he was about, then he didn't have to suffer any consequences if he was wrong. The fact that the old man was not confiding in him now came as no surprise. He didn't expect to be let in on it until Pop was ready to tell all. He had not always had such patience, but over the years he had learned that patience was indeed a virtue where Pop was concerned.

The old man took off toward the door at what was his approximation of a run which was really no more than a fast shuffle. To the casual observer, the sight would be, no doubt, a very ludicrous-looking scene, something like a floppy-footed clown trying to race in ridiculously oversized shoes.

Macklin followed him at a fast walk through the door and into the parking lot next to the courthouse.

Riley, at that moment, pulled up in one of the patrol cars. The stout deputy stepped out of the car on the driver's side and looked across the roof at the two of them. Even at that distance, Macklin could see the wonder in Riley's eyes. The old man, seeing Riley, shambled in his running shuffle toward the car.

Over his shoulder he yelled at Macklin. "Foller us." He jerked the patrol car door open and climbed into the front seat. Riley slid in on the other side and the car leaped into motion with tires squealing a protest. Seconds later Macklin heard the wailing roar of a siren and before they got completely out of sight, he saw the blue lights flashing their warning.

He ran to his Pontiac, slid inside, and swung the car in a hard, vicious turn and went racing out onto Harrison Street in pursuit of Riley. He pulled the magnet-based red light from its position on the console between the seats and shoved it out on the car's roof. He flipped a switch and his siren shrieked loudly. Threading traffic carefully, he topped the last rise which started the long decline leading down to the river. Most of the traffic had moved to the side of the street in response to the wailing sirens and he could see the patrol car, blue lights flashing, far ahead of him. He eased the accelerator down a bit more and felt the car lurch ahead. The patrol car, still far in front of him, made a careening turn into old Main Street and then headed north.

Macklin eased his Pontiac into Old Main, cut the siren, and pulled the flashing red light in off the roof. There wasn't enough traffic on Old Main to warrant using the warning device, and he soon ran off the tarmac and onto the gravel road that ran north along the flood plain.

The houses that were nestled among the trees that grew in scattered areas along the flood plain were, for the most part, old and rundown. As far as he knew, there were no blacks in this neighborhood but there were plenty of poor whites. Very possibly that fact ruled out Carl Watkins as the culprit. Occasionally, along the river one could find a fishing camp belonging to the more well-to-do in Cape Collins. In fact, in recent years, more and more of those who could afford two residences were building new places or remodeling old ones out along the river so they could have a place to go and rough it for the weekend or for the summer. Those who wanted to get away from town for a few days or even a few weeks found the flood plain an ideal place to own property.

It must be Gulf, he thought uncertainly. Gulf was the most likely candidate of the five suspects to have the means to afford a second place along the river. Although he really had no way of knowing how well fixed any of them were. It was conceivable that any one of the suspects could own a place out here. Another thought struck him. It was even more conceivable that the murderer rented rather than owned a place along the River. But, even so, I'll still put my money on Gulf, he thought. After all he had the Vaseline, and Macklin had decided that the killer had used the Vaseline.

Up ahead he saw a wink of brake lights as the patrol car vanished around a curve. He slowed the Pontiac in an effort to prevent it from fishtailing as he maneuvered through the curve. Despite his slowing, he went zooming past the patrol car, which had turned into a nearly hidden driveway. He hit the brakes hard and the car fishtailed and skidded to a stop. He threw the car in reverse and backed up sufficiently to allow him to pull in behind the patrol car.

Riley and Pop were out examining a Buick LeSabre that was parked in the yard. He slid out of his car and hurried to join them.

There was an old house which may originally have been an A-frame but it had been modified so much by additions that it was difficult to identify the original architecture anymore. The yard that surrounded the house was, in turn, surrounded by woodland composed mostly of hardwood trees. Thick underbrush grew amongst the trees and from where they stood, the river was not visible.

Just then there was a loud crack and a tinkling of glass as a rifle bullet ploughed into the headlight of the Buick.

Riley moved quickly and grabbed Pop, pulling him to safety on the other side of the squad car.

"Well, he knows we're here," Pop said. "And that's a rifle, you can bet on that."

Riley nodded his head in silent agreement. And if any one of them could identify a rifle from its sound, Riley, with all of his time in the arm, sure could. Macklin felt confident of that.

Pop tilted his cap forward over his forehead and scratched the thatch behind his right ear. He seemed to be deep in thought, assessing the situation. Riley was kneeling near the front fender of the prowl car, studying the house. Macklin stood back, waiting for Pop to come to a decision and outline his plan of attack.

Another shot reverberated through the quiet air and furrowed into the dirt behind them. Then three more shots followed quickly, each going harmlessly over their heads.

"Riley, you go that way," Pop said, pointing north along the road. "Macklin, you go the other way," he said, pointing south. "Circle around behind the house and see if you can get in the back door. The trees should give you enough cover if you're careful. I'll hold the fort here." He reached into the patrol car and withdrew the riot gun.

"You keep your head down," Macklin said as he started down the road. He walked along the road for about fifty yards, then cut into the woods.

He found the going difficult in among the trees. The briars and brambles and other low vegetation seemed to be everywhere, blocking his path. Guessing, he figured the thorn vines to be blackberry or raspberry plants but without the berries he really couldn't say for sure. Suddenly, a volley of shots rang out breaking the infernal quiet. He counted them automatically. There were six of them. He didn't reflect on them, but merely concentrated on making his way through the jungle of vegetation.

After what seemed to be an interminable length of time, he reached a position where he could plainly see the backdoor. The backyard was enclosed by a chest-high wire fence with two strands of barb-wire running along the top. There were four windows on the back of the house facing the river. One window was upstairs on the near side, and another one was positioned directly below it. Probably bedroom windows, he surmised. Another window, small in size and up high, was located on the far side. He guessed that to be a kitchen window. The last window of the four occupied the upper half of the backdoor and, unlike the others, had no curtains over it. Three plain wooden steps led up to the door.

He studied the windows intently but saw no movement. In fact, there was nothing about the windows that indicated to him that the backyard was being watched. He withdrew his pistol from the holster at his side and checked the loads. Cautiously, in a low crouch, he approached the fence and surveyed the windows again. Still he saw nothing moving—nothing to make him believe he was in any immediate danger. Carefully, he placed the heel of his hand on top of a wooden fence post and, using his arm as a lever, he easily vaulted over the fence. Immediately, he went into a crouch, clutching the revolver tightly. He ran his eyes over the windows once more, then surveyed the backyard. Where in hell was Riley? He should have been here by now. He looked around again. Well, he knew he couldn't stand here in the open all day waiting for Riley. The person in the house could appear at any one of those windows and he had no cover whatsoever.

Crouching low, he ran toward the house, expecting a shot at any minute. Five yards away from the house, he hit the dirt and rolled over and over until he came up against the foundation of the house near the steps on the knob side of the door.

He glanced around once more as if he expected the killer to appear out of thin air, then he checked the loads in the revolver again.

Where is Riley? he thought. Surely, he should have been here by now. Well, I can't wait forever. Jill is in there, and he was banking that she was still alive. Then he remembered the volley of shots that had rang out just a few minutes ago. It occurred to him that the killer was shooting at something, possibly Riley. He had to be firing at someone, and there was no one here but Pop, Riley and himself, and no one had fired at him. There had not been any return fire at that time nor since. All the shots had come from the same rifle. It struck him that he might be the only one left to face that maniac inside and rescue Jill. Well, he'd wait a few more minutes just in case Riley was having trouble getting through the undergrowth or was pinned down somewhere. Inside, it was going to require two people. One to draw fire from the killer and the other to take him.

His mind turned to whom might be waiting for him inside. He wished he'd have asked Pop who it was before he'd gotten himself in this predicament. It would be so much easier to storm the house if he knew who was in there. Once again he assessed the five suspects and eliminated Betty Landsberg immediately. It had to be a man, he thought. Of the remaining four, Gulf still seemed to be the most likely candidate. Now what? If it were Gulf how would he approach the situation differently from any of the others? Watkins, he had seen, was impulsive and quick to anger. If he had his choice Watkins was the one he'd most like to go up against. Rollins seemed indifferent. Very likely he would remain calm in any kind of confrontation. That would make Rollins difficult to go up against. A thinking man was always more difficult to take than one that acted on impulse. He thought of Rathlich but quickly eliminated him too. Rathlich was too sheepish to be able to function in this type of situation. . .or was he? Maybe the cowardly image he showed outwardly was just a facae. No. No, he had to be the coward he appeared to be. At least he had to go on that assumption. That left Gulf. Gulf appeared to be level-headed but also quick to anger. If it were Gulf, his best bet was to do something to throw him into a fit of rage, then he might possibly make a mistake which would give him an edge in the coming confrontation. He felt sure now that it was Gulf waiting for him in there. Yet, he'd still have to play it by ear and take the breaks as they came. Having decided on Gulf, he'd felt better about going into the house after him.

Damnit! Where was Riley? He looked again at the woods on the north side as if he expected Riley to appear at any moment. Riley had to be dead or severely wounded. He checked the revolver again.

Slowly, he inched his way upward to a semi-crouched position where he could reach the door knob. Gingerly, he twisted it. Then he threw the door open wide and pounded up the three steps and bowled inside.

The door opened onto a small foyer, and four more steps led up to a doorway opening on the kitchen. Quietly, he moved up the steps and glanced about the room. A U-shaped bank of cupboards faced him along three walls. On his left, toward the front of the house, was an old refrigerator with a chipped-enamel coating. Directly across from the refrigerator on his right, was an old gas range in a condition similar to the refrigerator.

Carefully, he peered around the door jamb, through the archway, toward the front of the house. Nothing stirred. It was just too quiet to suit him. Butterflies fluttered inside his stomach although he could have sworn they felt more like bat wings beating against his innards. His heart was thumping wildly, and he felt a tiny flicker of fear ignite in his breast and begin to grow. He swallowed back the lump in his throat and made up his mind to move.

Gathering himself, he dove across the floor and came

to rest up against the front of the refrigerator. He was sweating profusely and the palms of his hands were clammy. He laid the gun down and rubbed his hands vigorously on his shirt front.

He peered around the edge of the refrigerator. There was another doorway which opened onto a hall running east-west through the middle of the house. From his vantage point in the kitchen, he could see a stairway leading to the second floor. Obviously the hall connected bedrooms at either end of the house, and the stairs must lead to at least one room on the second story of the house. The killer could be in any one of those rooms, upstairs or down.

His heart was still fluttering, and he felt clammy all over. A sudden chill raced along his spine as he thought of that one-eyed rifle barrel staring at him dead center. Unsure of himself, he cowered back further behind the refrigerator and glanced at the back door as if he were still in hopes of seeing Riley come bursting through at any moment to assist him.

She was in there somewhere in one of those rooms. More than likely upstairs. At least if he were going to hold a captive in this house, he'd hold her upstairs. Of course, Jill had to be alive. She just had to be. Now, if Jill were upstairs did that mean that Gulf was upstairs too? Most probably he decided. If the killer were upstairs, he could keep an eye on his prisoner and at the same time watch the front approach to the house. He'd just have to gamble that his man was indeed in that upstairs bedroom.

Flattening himself against the floor, he belly-crawled, using his elbows to propel himself, through the arch, past the hall door to the partition separating the living room from the hall. Crouching up against the partition with a lamp-topped end table behind him, he peeked into the hall. From this viewpoint, he could no longer see the stairs but he could see that a bathroom with door ajar was situated right next to the stairs. He glanced at the living room. It was filled with old furniture, chipped and worn. Stained wallpaper covered the walls.

Dropping once again to a prone position, he crawled into and down the hall to the front bedroom. Slowly, he rose to a crouching position and surveyed the room. It smelled musky, and dust covered everything. Obviously, it hadn't been used in quite some time.

His man had to be upstairs. He already had ruled out the back bedroom as being too far from the action so that left only the upstairs and that made getting at him difficult.

Silence reigned. There had not been a noise made within the house other than those noises made by himself since he'd been in it—not a scrape nor a thump had been heard. There was nothing to identify where the man was hiding. But Gulf must know he was in the house. He just had to be waiting patiently until he made his move—waiting for him to come after him. He tried again to swallow the fear that gripped him but he was unsuccessful. It held him in its powerful grasp and was not about to let him go. As quietly as possible he crept back down the hall to his former position near the partition to make plans for storming the upstairs.

If it weren't for Jill being held prisoner, he could just wait him out. He had to find out if Jill were still alive and soon. He'd already taken too much precious time. The thought of her lying dead made him shudder, and it turned some of his fear into nervous anxiety. Was the killer anxious? Was he afraid, or was he just calmly waiting for him to poke his head up those stairs?

It really didn't matter how the killer felt. He was going to have to force a play. He checked his revolver for the umpteenth time. It was a poor choice to go up against a rifle with but it was the only weapon he had. Maybe at close range it would give him some sort of small advantage. He certainly hoped so, because he was at a disadvantage in every other way.

He peered around the partition and studied the stairs up as far as he could see. There was nothing he could see—no movement, no shadows—just nothing at all. That bastard was just setting there waiting for him like a hunter waiting for a rabbit to stick his head out of a hole in the ground.

There! What was that! He strained, listening intently. He was sure he'd heard a whimper. God! Now he was hearing things. But if it was a whimper he had heard, it might mean that Jill was indeed alive and well. He had to act and right now.

Dropping to a prone position once more, he elbowed his way across the hall to the foot of the stairs. Looking up, he could see the ceiling and a small part of the walls in the upstairs room. Still there was no movement—nothing to give him any idea as to which side of the stairwell the bastard was sitting on. He'd have to take his chances. He just knew he was going to get shot but, if it were face to face, he'd have a good chance of getting the sonofabitch before he died. Damn! He sure hated to get shot in the back but it was a possibility. What a waste getting shot in the back would be. He'd just have to guess right for Jill's sake if not his own. If he were shot in the back, Jill would die anyway.

Slowly, he inched up the stairs, keeping his back to the lefthand wall, thankful that the handrail was on the other side. As he moved upward more and more of the room came into view.

Then, just as he was about to make his move, he saw the rifle barrel with its one eye staring right at him. He froze! He couldn't move, could't bring his gun up to bear on the killer. All he could do was stand in a half crouch and stare at the rifle barrel. To him the whole scene seemed to last an eternity when in reality it all took place in a matter of seconds. Everything was in extremely slow motion.

There was a thunderous roar, and he felt a smashing impact against his right thigh which slammed him up against the stairwell. The pain had been quick and sharp but now his leg was numb. He found himself at the bottom of the stairs unaware that he had fallen. Quickly, he scuttled back to the kitchen.

Temporarily safe, he examined the injured leg. Red blood was slowly but steadily staining his khaki trouser leg. He jerked off his tie and tied it as tight as he could around his thigh above the wound. It was still welling blod but not as rapidly.

Christ! What did he do now? The bastard would be waiting for him. All he had to do was wait and pick him off at his leisure. He knew he would be coming and as soon as he stuck his head above the upstairs floor level, he'd blow him away with that rifle. Well, he couldn't wait. He was losing too much blood and he'd be too weak to move before long. He stood up, being careful to keep the refrigerator between him and the stairwell. He tested the leg and found he could put his weight on it. Good, nothing was broken but it had started to ache with a sharp, throbbing pain.

On all fours he crawled to the foot of the stairs again.

Suddenly, it occurred to him that he still didn't know who was waiting for him up there. The shock had been so great that all he had seen was that huge hole in the end of the rifle barrel staring at him. He still didn't know if it were Gulf or one of the others. Well, it didn't really make any difference now. Whoever it was up there he'd have to kill him. If he didn't he and Jill were both as good as dead.

He searched the top of the stairwell. But it was like it was before. There was nothing to indicate to him anything about which side the killer was waiting on for him. Damn, what a time to get buck fever, but then he'd never had to shoot a man before. What if it happened again? No, it had to be different this time. The sonofabitch was sure going to shoot him when the chance arose, so he'd best make the first shot count.

The last time he'd been on the west side of the room near the front window. That left the south and east sides as possibilities. What would he do if it were him being stalked? He couldn't be sure but he had to out guess the bastard or it was going to be all over. Meanwhile, his life was slowly leaking out of the hole in his leg.

He's gonna be on the same side of the room because he's gonna think I expect him to be on the other side of the room—the east, he told himself. He felt better now that he'd made a decision, and he hoped to God it was the right one.

Slowly, he inched up the first two steps. Then bracing himself, he exploded up the rest of the way, and as soon as the revolver had cleared the edge of the stairwell he began firing. The rifle roared close to him and he felt the force of the impact as the slug smashed the railing behind his head.

Sometime later he became aware that he was standing

there repeatedly pulling the trigger of an empty gun. How long he'd stood there that way he had no idea.

He holstered the empty revolver and walked over to peer down at Arthur Brockner. He was surprised at finding Brockner there instead of Gulf, or even one of the others, for that matter. He noticed that all six bullets had struck Brockner in the chest and that he was dead.

Turning, he saw Jill spread-eagled on a single bed. Her ankles and wrists were tied at the four corners of the bed and a gag was tied tightly around her head. She was looking at him with a mixture of relief and concern in her green eyes.

"Are you all right?" he asked.

She did her best to nod her head but she had difficulty.

He moved over to the bed and dug a knife out of his pocket and opened it. He cut the bindings on her wrists and ankles, examined the gag knot, then carefully sliced through the material and removed the gag.

She sat up, digging a mass of wadded rag out of her mouth. "God, Leonard. Am I glad to see you. I thought he'd killed you after that first shot. I think maybe he thought so too." She was rubbing her wrists, trying to get the circulation going again.

"Tell me about it, Jill," he said. "What happened to you anyway?"

"Are you sure you are all right? That wound looks mighty ugly and it's still bleeding."

"I'm okay," he said. He had taken a seat beside her on the bed.

"Well, I thought I'd offer myself as bait just to see if he'd come after me. I felt that I could take care of myself if I came face to face with him. We had no reason to believe he was armed and I had a gun. Any-

205

way, I parked my car at the shopping center. I guess I thought I could fool him that way."

"Gee, that was dumb," Macklin said. "Why didn't you tell me or Riley or somebody what you were planning to do?"

"You would have just tried to talk me out of it, so hush now and let me tell it."

"All right. Go ahead. Everything turned out all right."

"Well, it was about ten-thirty when I went up there. There wasn't anybody around. I walked around the science building and back and forth across the bridge. He must have seen me because when I went down in the ditch he was waiting for me. I didn't hear a thing. He just grabbed me and choked me with his forearm across my throat. Oh, I was so scared and I just knew he was going to kill me. Then I lost consciousness. I woke up in the backseat of his car and we were headed this way. My hands were tied behind my back."

She placed her hands on her knees and stretched her back.

"When we got here he hit me behind the ear with his hand and it knocked me out again. I woke up here. He was gone and didn't come in until early this morning. He checked my bonds but didn't say anything.

"He came back about mid-morning. He wasn't here long when he fired that first shot, then I knew Pop had finally figured out who had done it, and I knew you were here to rescue me. Oh, Leonard." She threw her arms around Macklin's neck and he held her close.

"Did he try to rape you?"

"No. He didn't make any sexual advances at all. Oh, he had his hand over my breast once while he was carrying me, but I'm sure it was accidental and not on purpose."

The creaking of a door opening downstairs drew their attention. Macklin stood up and started toward the stairs. When everything began to fade, he reached out for the railing. He thought he heard a scream far away and he sensed that he was falling but before he hit the floor, his world had turned to a dark black void.

23

Leonard Macklin opened his eyes and gradually became aware that he was no longer in the upstairs room in the old house near the river. Rather the antiseptic odor, the off-white walls, the television mounted on a rack near the far ceiling, and the console full of lights and buttons at his bedside told him he was in the hospital.

There was a dull, throbbing ache in his thigh. He ran a hand down under the covers and gingerly touched the bandages that swathed his leg.

At that moment a nurse came in. Her white, starched uniform flared out, emphasizing the curve of her hips. Golden curls nestled beneath a white cap with a back band which was perched near the back of her head.

"Well, you're awake at last. How do you feel?" she asked.

He folded his hands across his stomach. "My leg hurts like a damned toothache, and I feel a bit weak but otherwise I guess I'm okay," he said.

She checked the plastic IV bag that hung from a pole on his bed, adjusted the drip, and checked the tube where the needle entered a vein in his hand. Then she reached over and took his other hand, placing her fingers on his wrist, and began counting his pulse.

"You're lucky, you know," she said. "That bullet missed the bone and just knicked an artery. You're going to be all right." She dropped his wrist. "But that leg is going to be all stiff and sore for a while."

"How long have I been here?" he asked.

"The brought you in just a little after noon or so it says on your chart."

"What time is it now?"

She smiled. "Nearly seven."

She walked to the door, swung it open, then turned back toward him, holding the door with one hand.

"Say, there are some folks out here that would like to see you. I think they've been waiting all afternoon. Do you feel up to it?"

"Sure, send them in," he said. Suddenly, he felt good all over. A happy grin was stretched all over his face.

A few minutes later Pop, Jill and Riley trooped in. They each exchanged greetings with him, and Jill perched on the side of the bed. She took one of his hands and sandwiched it between hers. Pop sat in the only available chair, and Riley stood at the foot of the bed.

Macklin looked up at Riley's beefy face and said, "What happened to you, ole buddy? I thought you were gonna back me up."

Riley's face turned a cherry-red. "I got hung up in a goddamned bobwire fence. I was cuttin' through the woods and I came to this bobwire fence. When I tried to crawl through it, I got hung up. And the more I tried to get loose, the more entangled I got until I was tied up like a bulldogged calf. So I just hung there. I was scared to make much noise for fear that bastard would shoot me. I really didn't know if he could see me or not but I

209

wasn't takin' any chances. I finally yelped and Pop came to get me.''

"Yep," Pop said. "He was so tangled up we had to send to town for wire-cutters to get him out. I never seen the likes of it." Jill laughed, and Riley frowned.

Macklin looked over at Pop. "You know you never did tell me who it was in that house—who it was I had to take out. I didn't know who I was going up against until after he was already dead. I was real surprised it was Brockner."

"Hmm," Pop said. He slapped his knee. "Danged if I didn't forget. I reckon I just naturally assumed that when I come up with the feller's name that you fellers had too." He shrugged his shoulders.

Jill turned slightly so she could see Pop better.

"I still don't understand," she said. "I really can't see how Brockner was related to those two girls."

"I never even suspected Brockner," Macklin said.

Pop pursed his lips and ran a hand along the underside of his jaw. "Oh, I suspected Art all along but he was at the bottom of my list until this mornin'. Ya see, Brockner was a lonely old man with all the normal desires. I ain't sure he was ever married but that didn't mean he didn't have a normal sex drive. You see, he took pleasure from ogling the young gals. Most likely, he was undressin' them with his eyes. And he sure had a lot of young coeds to work with in that science building."

"Ah ha," Jill said.

"Right," Pop said. "Now Becky Mason noticed how he stared at them gals and figgered him for a dirty old man. You recollect, Len, that her pappy said she had a sadistic streak, and Gulf told us she was a sexual tease. Well, she decided she was gonna have some fun with that old man, and I reckon she teased him to distraction. Just how much we'll never know. Only trouble was she teased him once too often.''

"And he killed her," Jill said.

"Exactly," Pop said.

"But how did Melba Stuart fit into the picture?" Jill asked. "She was a nice girl. She certainly wasn't a tease."

"Yer right. The Stuart girl was a nice girl. But she was his big mistake," Pop said. "If he'd a quit after killin' the Mason gal we most likely would never have got him. Right from the first I figgered there was somethin' different about the second murder but I couldn't pin it down for a time. Then it occurred to me that probably the first murder was a spur of the moment thing, but the second showed all the signs of bein' intentional and well planned—too well planned.

"How could it have been well planned?" Jill asked. "Rollins told you that the Stuart girl had said that Gulf had called her and invited her over to the science building that night. Or was Rollins lying again?"

"Nope. He was tellin' straight facts as far as he knew 'em that time," Pop said. "But it wasn't Gulf that called her."

"But why did Rollins lie about the flat tire?" Macklin asked.

"Oh, he was havin' an affair with a gal name of Janice somethin' er other and he didn't want his wife to find out. I reckon he figgered we wouldn't check his story." Pop dug out his pipe, glanced around the room, then thought better of it and replaced the pipe in his sweater pocket.

"Wait a minute," Jill said. "What do you mean it wasn't Gulf that called. That girl knew Gulf well enough that she surely could recognize his voice over the telephone.''

"Nope," Pop said. "Wasn't Gulf. It was Brockner. Oh, she knew Gulf well enough but it wasn't him. Maybe you noticed if you talked to Brockner that he had a habit of talkin' in other people's voices, movie stars and the likes mostly. Well, back in the time when he was boxin' he used to do impressions. He was good enough to do some stage shows at the time. Fact is, he was probably good enough to have earned a livin' at it. Don't know why he never did. Anyhow, he was around Gulf enough to pick up his voice inflections and tonal qualities so that gal just naturally thought it was Gulf that called her.''

"Well, I'll be damned," Macklin said. "That sure makes sense now that you mention it."

"But what about the Vaseline?" Riley asked.

"Yes, what about the Vaseline?" Jill asked. "And who had sexual intercourse with those girls before Brockner killed them. It had to be the same man.''

"Hold on," Pop said. "You're askin' too many questions at once." He fidgeted, obviously missing his pipe. "The Vaseline was the first thing that set me on the track, although it led me astray for a while.''

"But I found the Vaseline in Gulf's desk," Riley said.

"Yep," Pop said. "It was planted there by Brockner. He saw that I was after Gulf pretty heavy so he gave me somethin' to build my suspicions on. In fact, it was my suspicions of Gulf that got the Stuart girl killed.''

"What!" Macklin said. "How could that be?"

"Brockner knew she had a crush on Gulf. So he planned her murder with the idea of trumpin' up enough circumstantial evidence to make Gulf look guilty. When that evidence begin to turn up, that's when

I backed off and took a good look at the whole thing. The Vaseline was the one that kicked it off."

"That explains the rubber heel marks on the floor. Brockner dragged the Stuart gal's body across the hall to make it look like Gulf had killed her in his office, then dragged her across to that janitor's storeroom."

"That's all fine conjecture," Jill said. "But who had sexual intercourse with those two girls before Brockner killed them. Certainly if Brockner had tried they would have resisted—struggled in some way. And if they had resisted, then Doc Spelchur would have found some evidence of forced entry—of rape."

"Good point, Jill," Macklin said.

"Nobody had sex with them gals before they died," Pop said, "except for the Mason girl. She'd had intercourse with the Rathlich kid, but him and Brockner had the same blood type and Doc missed that one."

"So what? You've sure got me puzzled," Jill said. "Rathlich didn't use Vaseline with Becky Mason yet it was there just like with Melba Stuart. I just don't understand."

"Brockner used the Vaseline," Pop said, chuckling at the girl's quandry. "Brockner had intercourse with the gals after he killed them. He used the Vaseline to replace the natural secretions that would have been there if they were alive. That way it didn't look like rape."

"My God!" Jill said. "A necrophile. How despicable!"

Macklin scratched his head with his free hand. He said, "It's all finally beginning to make sense. But I still don't see what tipped you off that it was Art Brockner."

"You recollect this mornin' when you was questionin' them suspects, and after it was over and

213

they had gone, I said somethin' about the key to it all. Well, that's when the missin' piece fell into place. A little somethin' Art said when we was over in the science buildin' that mornin' Melba Stuart was killed lit up in my mind like a neon sign.''

''I don't recall him saying anything that would point a finger at him,'' Macklin said.

''I don't either,'' Jill said. Riley just shrugged.

''He did, though,'' Pop said. ''It didn't mean much at the time, leastways it didn't register outloud to me then. He said somethin' like 'When I unlocked this mornin'.' In fact, he said it twice.''

''I don't see how that statement would incriminate Brockner,'' Macklin said.

''Well, seems as how the college is real careful about who they let have keys to the doors around here. If a key was to fall into a student's hands, it could create all sorts of problems, so they keep close tabs on their keys. Now, a professor would have a key that fits his office and the classrooms. A graduate student would have a key to his office, and apparently some of the chemistry majors have keys to the chemistry lab. That's because they have ongoing experiments which need attention at odd hours. Now, all of these keys fit the outside doors, of course. But—'' he hesitated for effect. ''None of 'em fit the janitor's storage closet. The only one with a key to all the doors was the janitor, Art Brockner.''

''Well, I'll be damned!'' Riley said.

Macklin nodded his head. ''I see it all now. Brockner's key was actually the key to murder so to speak.''

Pop just nodded in return.

''One thing,'' Macklin said. ''Why didn't he kill Jill like he did the others? He had plenty of chances.''

"Oh, that's easy," Jill said. "He was gonna pump me for information before he did me in. He wanted to know how close Pop was to guessing the truth. I think he would have killed me in short order if you hadn't turned up when you did, Leonard."

"Yep," Pop said. "We'll never know why he didn't kill you last night, I reckon. But he had to appear on the job this mornin' so as not to look suspicious. Maybe, he was just tryin' to think of what to do with the body."

Just then the door opened and Shirrell Olson walked in.

"How's the patient?" Olson asked.

"Oh, I'm a little weak, a little stiff and a little sore, but I'll but up and around before you know it. I can't let this old man solve crimes on his own."

The last drew a chuckle from everyone.

"Pop was just filling us in on all of the particulars of the case and how he found out it was Arthur Brockner."

"Good. Good. You'll have to come by my office and tell me all about the case in a day or two," Olson said.

"Am I still chief?" Pop asked, grinning widely.

Olson returned the grin. "You sure as hell are. Claude Dale has crawled back into his shell—temporarily at least. You know, he sort of reminds me of a whipped dog. Yes, sir. It will be awhile before Claude Dale bothers us again, I imagine."

Just then the nurse walked in. "I've overlooked the rules and let all of you people in here. Now, our patient needs his rest. You can all come and see him tomorrow."

With that they all said their goodbys to Macklin and left together.

Left alone, Macklin shook his head and said to

himself, "Damn, it's surprising how a little thing like priority can trip up what was almost the perfect murder."

THE SPANKING GIRLS
Carter Brown
BT51383 $1.50
Mystery

A beautiful porn star is murdered in the beach house of an eccentric millionaire who is known for his many marriages—always to virgins. Al Wheeler has to find out who the girl really is—and how she got there!

Setting: Southern California, contemporary

DONAVAN'S DELIGHT
Carter Brown
BT51382 $1.50
Mystery

With over 50,000,000 books in print, Carter Brown is one of the worlds most popular writers, and now he joins the Belmont/Tower line with a novel about a man who discovers that the stately manor next door is more sinister than it seems!

Setting: England, contemporary

DEADLY PARTY
Linda DuBreuil
BT51374 $1.50
Mystery

The Governor was a shoo-in for re-election, but it was getting dangerous to support him—his friends were being murdered. Was it a coincidence—or was it part of a more sinister conspiracy? Sloan Malone had to find out before he became the next victim!

Setting: Indiana, 1970's

REUNION
Richard Russell
BT51364 $1.50
Mystery

Davey had been dead a long time, but his teacher still wanted to find out who killed him. She hired Angel Graham—and then the teacher was murdered. The next victim was Gwen Queens, Angel's paramour, and Angel, with Gwen's brother Jeff, had a personal score to settle with the killer.

Setting: New York and New Jersey, contemporary

THE NIGHTMARE MACHINE   BT51372 $1.75
John Nicholas Datesh   Mystery

Suppose you dreamed that you were dying—and you
couldn't wake up? Raymond Carleton learned how to
control people's dreams. He was a genius, and venge-
ful. A little sleeping powder made him a murderer.
Montgomery had to stop him—but first he had to find
out how Carleton did it!
Setting: Pittsburgh, contemporary

GUILTY AS CHARGED   BT51373 $1.75
Elizabeth Hanley   Mystery

All the evidence was circumstantial—no one had
found Marge Ratliffe's body, nor could anyone say for
certain whether or not she was dead. But her husband
Cliff had pleaded guilty to the murder. Even so, some
people refused to believe him!
Setting: Illinois, 1930's

DEADLIER THAN
THE MALE   BT51160 $1.50
J. C. Conway   Mystery

Four men had been beheaded with no clues, no
motive, no suspect remaining. Novice Private
Investigator Jana Blake finds her first criminal case a
bizarre chain of killings with no real lead. Join Jana as
she takes her sleuthing from the subways of
Manhattan to its breathtaking conclusion in the sky
over the East River! A BT Original.

DOMINIQUE   BT51345 $1.50
R. Chetwynd-Hayes   Mystery

David Ballard didn't like living on his wife's
money—he wanted to make it his own. It was easy:
he drove her mad, then to suicide. But Dominique
didn't stay dead, and Ballard found himself trapped
in a maze of hallucinations and hauntings that left
him with no way out—except death!

MUSIC TO MURDER BY
BT51262 $1.75
Vernon Hinkle
Mystery

Sergeant Holliman chose his words carefully. "Mr. Webb has established himself in scholarly circles as a superior detective, having the knack for uncovering answers to questions that baffle his colleagues."

"Yes, but in the field of music," suggested Bimbo.

"His solutions are based on a superior intuition," continued Holliman. "In other words, he may be some sort of genius, and I'm ready to take a chance on him."

"Sergeant Holliman," asked Bimbo, "are you asking policemen to cooperate with a civilian rather than the other way around?"

"If you want to put on a uniform again," Holliman said, "cooperate with the librarian, and never breathe a word if he screws up!"

30 MANHATTAN EAST
BT51311 $1.75
Hillary Waugh
Mystery

Detective Frank Sessions worked out of Homicide North. He got the tough cases, and Monica Glazzard's murder was one of them. She was a gossip columnist with a lot of enemies—including her daughter. Sessions' problem was too many suspects!

A GRAVEYARD TO LET
BT51222 $1.50
Carter Dickson
Mystery

Sir Henry Merrivale had solved difficult cases in his long, distinguished career. But this was the most baffling! There was the strange matter of the graveyard—but that was only the beginning . . . A complicated puzzle by a master of mystery.

THE ANALOG BULLET
Martin Smith

BT51220 $1.50
Suspense

Newman ran for Congress, but the experts said he didn't have a chance. No one was more surprised than he was when the computers said he'd won—by a landslide! And computers don't lie—or do they? A political thriller about a young politician who became the victim of a terrifying conspiracy.

Martin Smith is an elegant writer."
—*New York Times*

FINISH ME OFF
Hillary Waugh

BT51324 $1.75
Mystery

Another Homicide North mystery! Someone had murdered a hooker, and Detective Frank Sessions had to find the killer before he struck again. But there were a lot of men in her life, and any one of them could have done it!

MINNESOTA STRIP
Peter McCurtin

BT51333 $1.75
Mystery

Tracing runaways was the kind of work private eye Pete Shay was used to. It was an easy seven hundred bucks when he took Janssen's money to find the missing Ruthie. He never expected to find himself on a murder case! A new novel from an Edgar Award-winning writer!

CROOKED LETTER
Linda DuBreuil

BT51385 $1.75
Mystery

Poison-pen letters were doing their work in Woodsdale, creating an atmosphere of suspicion and hate. Soon the murders began, the sheriff was killed, and the mystery was left to be solved by an alcoholic cripple!
Setting: Midwest, contemporary

HEROES DIE YOUNG

Rick Sandford

BT51361 $1.75

War

When Jeff Parton got to France he knew nothing about combat, and he figured he was lucky to have battle-hardened Gil Ryder for a buddy. Ryder would teach Parton what he needed to know to stay alive—and sooner or later this education would pay off!

Setting: France, 1944

MISSION INCREDIBLE

Lawrence Cortesi

BT51346 $1.50

War

The five-man crew of the downed B-25 survived the crash, but they were separated. Each one had to fight his way out of the New Guinea jungle alone. And when they got home each one had a different story to tell. Somewhere in those stories was the truth about a Japanese ambush!

Setting: New Guinea, World War II

ESPIONAGE

William S. Doxey

BT51363 $1.95

Spy

The leaks were impossible. The only way the Russians could have gotten the information they had was if they could read minds. James Madderly, parapsychologist, was given an order: Find out if it was true, and, if it was, stop it from happening again!

Setting: London, Finland, Leningrad, contemporary

MAYHEM ON THE CONEY BEAT

Michael Geller

BT51353 $1.75

Crime

Angel Perez took round one—he had Bud Dugan busted down from detective to patrolman. But Dugan wasn't throwing in the towel yet, and when his ex-partner was found dead—apparently of an overdose of heroin—Dugan was back on the case, with a big reason to nail the heroin kingpin Perez.

ONE OF OUR BOMBERS IS MISSING
Dan Brennan

BT51140　$1.50
Novel

A searing graphic account of an air mission over Europe in World War II.

"...one of the best, most moving war novels..."
— *Minneapolis Tribune*

"It is a moving salute to the heroes who nightly endure the tension and terrors that are here so graphically described...stark honesty and marked artistic skill."
— *Liverpool Evening Express*

THE CAMP
Jonathan Trask

BT51214　$1.50
Novel

A group of right wing military officers were running a top secret operation deep in the woods of New England. Its written purpose was to toughen soldiers against torture, but its real purpose was more nefarious... The Camp would threaten the very security of the United States. A BT Original.

DEADLY COMPANIONS
Bob Sang and Dusty Sang

BT51243　$1.50
Novel

Jacob Pendleton was a latter-day James Bond who would take on just about any dangerous job...provided the price was right. This latest assignment called for him to deposit a million dollars worth of gems in Vault Box 211 in a Geneva bank, and then to repeat the proceedings in banks all over the world. All within 72 hours, no questions asked. The Chicago-based adventurer knew he could get killed, but that was part of the job.

BOMBER RAID
James Campbell

BT51272 $1.75
War Novel

On the ground, the war was at a stalemate, but in the air the RAF and the Luftwaffe were battling every night over the cities of Germany. On both sides, men were trying to kill the enemy and stay alive, and their women waited to see if they would return. A novel with all the passion and drama of war itself, written by one of the men who lived it, a hero of the Battle of Britain.

ROGUE SERGEANT
Lawrence Cortesi

BT51352 $1.75
War

Mike Renna wasn't a model soldier. He'd been busted down from sergeant so often he should've had buttons on his stripes. He'd been wounded, gone AWOL, done everything a G.I. wasn't supposed to do. But when his unit needed him in the battle for France, Mike Renna showed his true colors—and became a hero!
Setting: Europe, 1944-45.
Author's Home: Watervliet, NY

SUCH ARE THE VALIANT
John C. Andrews

BT51314 $1.50
War

The Japanese conquerors had finally been stopped in Burma. Now a small band of soldiers, cut off from their own lines, had to turn the Japanese around— with nothing more than the help of a few Burmese and their own courage!

SEND TO: BELMONT TOWER BOOKS
P.O. Box 270
Norwalk, Connecticut 06852

Please send me the following titles:

Quantity	Book Number	Price
_____	_____	_____
_____	_____	_____
_____	_____	_____
_____	_____	_____
_____	_____	_____

In the event we are out of stock on any of your selections, please list alternate titles below.

_____	_____	_____
_____	_____	_____
_____	_____	_____
_____	_____	_____

Postage/Handling _____

I enclose..... _____

FOR U.S. ORDERS, add 50¢ for the first book and 10¢ for each additional book to cover cost of postage and handling. Buy five or more copies and we will pay for shipping. Sorry, no C.O.D.'s.

FOR ORDERS SENT OUTSIDE THE U.S.A.
Add $1.00 for the first book and 25¢ for each additional book. PAY BY foreign draft or money order drawn on a U.S. bank, payable in U.S. ($) dollars.

☐ Please send me a free catalog.

NAME _____
(Please print)

ADDRESS _____

CITY _____ STATE_____ ZIP _____
Allow Four Weeks for Delivery